Praise for *The Pickup Artist*

"Bisson can charm your toes off."
—*The Washington Post Book World*

"Masterfully ironic, *The Pickup Artist* has enough that's funny and foolish to keep readers laughing as the shelves and walls and boxes are cleared."
—*The Philadelphia Inquirer*

"Readers familiar with Bisson's earlier fine novels . . . will appreciate his odd combination of the comfortably domestic and the faintly grotesque. . . . [It] offers a succession of pleasures and manages to do something startling every time you think you have taken its measure."
—*The Star-Ledger* (New Jersey)

"This is science fiction as satire at its best. If Ray Bradbury had cowritten *Fahrenheit 451* with Jonathan Swift, they might have come up with something like *The Pickup Artist*. Grade: A."
—*Rocky Mountain News*

"With *The Pickup Artist*, a cockeyed fable about art and obsolescence, Terry Bisson . . . walks in the footsteps of Ray Bradbury and Kurt Vonnegut. . . . *The Pickup Artist* provides plenty of sharp-eyed satire and droll characterizations."
—*San Francisco Chronicle*

"Science fiction needs humor, and it is plentiful in this zany, serio-comic variation on Ray Bradbury's *Fahrenheit 451*."
—*Publishers Weekly*

"From page one on, things get curiouser and curiouser in Bisson's second novel, which in its blend of the eerie, sexy, and the disgusting . . . becomes surrealistic in the manner of a Buñuel movie. If this gets filmed, though, the Coen brothers should do it."
—*Booklist* (starred review)

"Terry Bisson's latest book is a laugh-out-loud fantastic tale. . . . Bisson enters the land of Vonnegut, Douglas Adams, and even Ray Bradbury's *Fahrenheit 451*. . . . This novel is mordantly funny, fast-moving, and sharp. If, as he claims, Kurt Vonnegut really has given up writing novels, we can relax a bit—Terry Bisson will keep us on our toes."
—*Bookpage*

TOR BOOKS BY TERRY BISSON

Bears Discover Fire and Other Stories
Pirates of the Universe
In the Upper Room and Other Likely Stories
The Pickup Artist

THE PICKUP ARTIST

Terry Bisson

A TOM DOHERTY ASSOCIATES BOOK NEW YORK

THE PICKUP ARTIST

Copyright © 2001 by Terry Bisson

This book is printed on acid-free paper.

Edited by David G. Hartwell

Book design by Jane Adele Regina

A Tor Book
Published by Tom Doherty Associates, LLC
175 Fifth Avenue
New York, NY 10010

www.tor.com

Tor® is a registered trademark of Tom Doherty Associates, LLC.

Library of Congress Cataloging-in-Publication Data

Bisson, Terry.
    The pickup artist / Terry Bisson.
        p. cm.
    "A Tom Doherty Associates book."
    ISBN 0-312-87403-0 (hc)
    ISBN 0-312-87421-9 (pbk)
        1. Art and state—Fiction. 2. Government investigators—Fiction.
    I. Title.

PS3552.I7736 P54 2001
813'.54—dc21   00-053217

First Hardcover Edition: April 2001
First Trade Paperback Edition: April 2002

Printed in the United States of America

0 9 8 7 6 5 4 3 2 1

For David Hartwell,
the good genie

THE
PICKUP ARTIST

Chapter 1

Everybody has one thing they keep, one thing that matters to them more than anything else. Life is just a process of elimination, figuring out what that one thing is. You may figure it out right at the end, just as you're losing it. If you're lucky.

The day I began to figure it out, for that's how I think of it now, was a Monday and it started like any other, except backwards. Homer usually wakes me up, not the other way around. I heard the *beep beep* of my slate in the other room and realized I had been hearing it for a while. Had I been only dreaming I was still asleep?

I had to pee and in dreams I don't have to pee. Then I thought: where *is* that dog?

"Homer?" Usually the slate wakes her up right away, like an alarm. I get something from the Bureau every day, even if it's just a no-go. I was about to call her again when I heard the clicking of big paws on the bare wood floor, and there she was, licking my face. Her breath smelled a little worse than usual, but her beady, black eyes were bright. I got up to pee and make her breakfast (my coffee makes itself) and saw that it was already seven.

Not that it mattered. Mondays were light.

I took Homer for her walk, then tossed slate and bag into the lectro and hit the road. The first pickup was in a nice neighborhood on the back side of Todt (on Staten Island it's pronounced "toad") Hill. From the top you can see Manhattan and Brooklyn: one tall, one short; one near, one far; both looking uncluttered and clean. And the Atlantic to the east, as flat and featureless as the prairie in a dream. I often dreamed about the West in those days. That was before my dreams came true.

The house was about halfway down the hill, on a winding, leafy street. We're not allowed to reveal names or addresses, of course. I parked right in front. There was a dog on the porch, a mutt, looking dangerous but sleepy. The door was opened by a fat White guy in a tee shirt and jeans, not nearly as nice as his house. His shirt said: SO?

I showed him my slate and he looked at it uncomprehendingly. Truly uncomprehendingly. I've known pickups to fake ignorance, but his was the real thing.

"So?"

"I expect you know why I'm here."

"Help me out," he said. "BIA? Bureau of Indian Affairs?"

"B-*A-E*," I said. "Arts and Entertainment."

"Oh, yeah. You are the guys who pick up old stuff."

"Right," I said, though there's a lot more to the Bureau than that. "You think you might invite me in? It's a little nippy out here."

Only a little: it was mid-October. But the first thing we learn at Academy is that things go easier if you can get your foot in the door. Mr. SO? grumbled a little and stepped back out of the way. We both sat down on the same stiff couch, facing the same cluttered coffee table. It was awkward, but I'm used to that. I'm aware that we're dealing with more than just stuff: it's memories, dreams, and, of course, money.

"Does the name Miller, Walter M., Jr., mean anything to you?" I asked. The idea is to give the pickup every opportunity to volunteer.

"Miller? Jr.? Sure. Sci-fi writer, *Canticle for Leibowitz*, wasn't it? Mid-century, back when books were . . . wait a minute! You mean Miller was deleted?"

"Six weeks ago," I said.

"I didn't know he had been pulled. I don't keep up with science fiction anymore. Or even science."

"I know what you mean," I said. If he was going to be agreeable, I wasn't going to argue.

"So? Oh. I get it. I must have one of his paperbacks. I thought they were still legal. To tell you the truth, I haven't looked through them in over a year. They're not really a collection. They're sort of a leftover. I guess this is my lucky day."

"That's right," I said. We pay 125 for each pickup. People who don't know anything about us, know that.

"And Arthur's unlucky day."

"Walter," I said. Then I gave him what I call the Academy answer: "He had his day in the sun. Now it's someone else's turn."

"Sure, whatever," Mr. SO? said sourly. He disappeared into another room and I could hear him opening and closing drawers. I kept my eye on the door, just in case. He came back with a box half filled with paperback books. Maybe two-thirds. Just enough so that they halfway stood up.

He had to sort through them all; they weren't in any particular order. "Maybe there are some others in here," he said.

"I wouldn't know about that," I said. "I just have my list. You can check the Bureau's website. Any that you take in yourself are worth an extra fifty."

"Or five hundred from a bootlegger," he said. "Or five thousand. I saw that story about what's his name, Salinger."

"I wouldn't know about that," I said. "And I'm required by law to remind you that it's against the law to even joke about bootleggers."

A chill fell over the room. I didn't mind. You can't get too chummy; you have to remind people that you work for the government.

"Whatever," he said. "Here he is. So long, Arthur. Walter."

He flipped me the book. It had a hooded monk on the cover. The pages fanned out and it hit the floor. I picked it up off the dingy rug and dropped it into my bag.

"Aren't you even going to look at it? Read a word of it? Before you destroy it? You might learn something about life."

"Nobody gets destroyed," I said. With my fingertip I scored him off my slate and punched in 125.

"It's not just a book you're wiping out. It's a human life!"

He was starting to get belligerent. It was time to go. I stood up. "I don't get involved with all that. I just pick up the stuff and send it to Worth Street."

"And then?"

"And then, who knows?" I reached for his hand. "Thanks for your cooperation."

He wouldn't shake my hand. "So long, Walter," he said, to my bag. His eyes were shining.

I began to back toward the door. Sentimentality and violence are closely allied. We learn that at Academy. We like to joke that our job is half diplomacy, half psychology, half math.

"What about the money?" he growled as I opened the door. I heard an answering growl from the porch.

"I've already put it into your account. Your cooperation is much appreciated."

"Oh, well," he said. "I guess you're just doing your job. I guess it's discouraging to the new writers to have the old ones hanging around forever."

Sarcasm or sudden friendliness? Either way, it's another bad sign. "Forever was never exactly the deal anyway," I said, closing the screen door behind me and backing slowly off the porch, watching the dog. They pick up their clues from the owners.

"Too bad for Miller he's not a fucking Movie Star! Huh?"

I left him shouting through the screen. I was down the steps, on the street, in the lectro and gone. My second pickup was down on the flats near South Beach, in one of those neighborhoods with tiny wooden houses and crumbly sidewalks made with too much sand.

Turned out this pickup *was* a Movie Star: or at least a

movie. We hear the movie star comment a lot. Some people don't think it's fair for movies (and not stars) to be pulled, while writers are taken out as individuals. And I guess it's not. I can't really argue with them. Not that I would anyway. It's not my place to argue.

A woman came to the door. About sixty, but dressed like twenty going on forty. The room was dark and the TV was blaring—one of those daytime talk shows where half the guests are cartoon characters from the prime-time shows, who don't depress the cushions on the couches.

Mrs. 20/40 hit MUTE and invited me in as soon as I showed her my badge. The pickup was a VHS, pre-DVD, still in its little box, complete with a color picture. The hat, gun, and horse identified it as a Western.

"I meant to take this in," she said. "I was going to take it in last week, but my car broke down."

She didn't look like she had a car, or even a lectro, to me. My guess was, she'd heard we had discretionary. I didn't care; it's not my money, and I like to accommodate people whenever I can (especially after that last pickup!).

"I understand," I said as I dropped the movie into my bag and said, "Tell you what. I'll put you down for the extra fifty. Since you tried to bring it in."

"Problem is," she said, "I don't have a bank account. Maybe I could get cash?"

I didn't believe that one either. I knew, and she knew I knew, she was trying to avoid the tax. But again, what did I care? She handed me her card and I ran it through my slate.

"You're a prince," she said.

"Not at all," I said. "Just a pickup artist doing his job."

"A what?"

"A pickup artist. It's just a term we use."

Well, if it ain't Santa," said Lou, the bartender at Ducks & Drakes, where I usually, actually always, went for lunch in those days. A bud with tomato juice, plus a raw egg on the side. I am pretty health conscious. Or rather, was.

Lou called me Santa because I always brought in the bag. I didn't feel comfortable leaving it in the lectro. And it was big, as big as a postman's bag, with the BAE seal on it and everything.

"What's the damage today?" he asked.

I opened the bag and let Lou look in with the little flashlight he keeps behind the bar—the one he shines in your face when you've had too much to drink, and says, "That's all, folks." As long as he doesn't reach into the bag or touch anything, it's not technically a violation.

Lou shrugged and said "Miller?" but he knew the movie. "Clint Eastwood," he said. "I didn't know he'd been pulled! My dad loved him. He named my older brother after him."

"Clint?"

"Woody."

"You might be thinking of Woody Harrelson," I said.

"Or Woody Allen," said a voice from the dark end of the bar. Dante, or at least that's what Lou calls him. He's a retired cop or something; always sitting there in the gloom. "You pull movies but not Movie Stars. So how come a singer disappears as soon as his number comes up?"

"Come on!" said Lou. "They can't pull Movie Stars because they are never in movies alone. You would have the other actors talking to a blank spot on the screen."

"So? Singers aren't on CDs alone either."

"Sometimes they are," Lou said. "Besides, movies are different. Movies would last forever unless they were pulled. They would clog up the world like cholesterol."

"The singer thing eats shit," said Dante. "They never should have pulled Sinatra. He was a Movie Star, too."

"It's all politics," said Lou, cracking an egg into my glass. "Right, Shapiro? Movies have clout. Buzz. Whang. Pizzazz. Besides, this other guy is a mystery writer, not a singer, right, Shapiro?"

"Science fiction," I said.

"Same thing," Dante said from the gloom. "Another thing, how come they're always picking on Italians?"

"Maybe it's because you Italians are complaining all the time," Lou said. "Right, Shapiro?"

"Whatever," I said. At Academy we're trained not to argue and it carries over into private life. But sometimes the stuff people say gets to me. In the first place, the Bureau doesn't pull anybody unless they're already dead. In the second place, it's done by a random generator, and Dante knows that. And in the third place, who says Clint Eastwood was Italian anyway?

I only had one pickup that afternoon. It was on a street right off Silver Lake. I parked a block away and took my time.

I love Silver Lake. It's like a mirror image of the world, with houses, trees, cars, all around the edges—and in the center, a blue hole, the empty sky. I often think (thought) of my job that way. The Bureau was the blue hole that kept everything else in order.

The house was an ancient "ranch-style" with an attached garage, open and filled with junk. A toothless old dog came out and started to bark, then fell into step and walked me up to the porch. Some guys have a way with women, with kids, or with other guys. I have it with dogs.

The door was open except for a screen. The inside of the house was dark. No bell. I banged on the screen. The man who came to the door was tall and skinny, with long brown hair brushed across a bald crown.

I verified his name and showed him my slate, which had my badge for a screensaver. I told him what I was after.

Mr. Baldy didn't try the blank look thing. Just invited me in. Kept the dog out with the screen door.

I sat down with my bag at my side in a dark living room.

The drapes and the rug matched; they looked like they hadn't been cleaned in years. Mr. Baldy excused himself and returned a few minutes later with a square, flat cardboard folder with a picture on it of a cowboy getting into (or out of) a car: a record album. The disk inside it was like a CD but much, much bigger, and two-sided, with tiny grooves. "This is what you want," he said. "It's an LP."

"I know, I've seen them," I said. Not literally true, but at Academy we covered all the twentieth-century storage and retrieval media. There are so many different types it's covered in two separate courses.

"Mind if I listen to it one last time?"

I was so curious I almost said yes. Particularly when I saw the playback device. It was a box with a lid—a record-player. He had opened it and set the turntable spinning, before I came to myself and said, "Sorry, but we're strictly not allowed."

"I get it," he said, closing the lid. Though exactly what he got I couldn't say. I was holding the LP, staring at the picture of the cowboy—you could tell by the hat—standing beside a car, holding a guitar.

"Are you okay?"

"I guess," I said. I stuck the LP into my bag. "Sure."

"You looked for a minute there like you were about to cry."

"Just a long day," I said, even though it was only two in the afternoon. I wiped my eyes and was surprised to feel tears on the back of my hand.

"So long, Hank," he said.

"Huh?"

"Hank Williams," he said. "One of the great ones. An immortal."

"I'm required by law to remind you that there aren't any Immortals," I said. "That proposal was defeated with the provision that . . ."

"Just an expression," he said. "No harm, okay?"

The dog wanted to follow me but I sent him into the garage. I took the long way back around the lake. I couldn't get that picture out of my head. It reminded   ι song. I could almost, but not quite, hear it in my he   ·

Plus there was the name, Hank. Though I ιι ʌer, ever use it, it's my first name. According to my mother, it's the name my father gave me.

Chapter 2

There was too much stuff.
    Everybody knew it, but nobody knew what to do about it.

The solution, or the Deletion Option, as it came to be called when it became official government policy, arrived with a bang, literally. On 5 Avril 20— at 4:04 a.m., a small explosion was followed by an intense blaze at the Musée d'Orsay in Paris. By the time the fire was contained, four impressionist masterpieces had been destroyed, including Monet's Railway at Argenteuil. The fire had been set by a small, timed incendiary device.

An email communiqué to the offices of Paris Match and The International Herald Tribune claimed responsibility for the attack by a group calling themselves "Les Eliminateurs." Identifying themselves only as an "international collective of artists," and using imagery that was at times shockingly vulgar, they compared Western culture to the human body and asked what would happen if one only ate and never eliminated.

The international nature of their movement was made apparent the next week, when two bombs exploded simultaneously in London's Tate Gallery and Madrid's Prado. The Tate fire was the most severe, damaging two Turners and destroying a Constable. The Prado was a misfire. Museums throughout Europe responded by replacing their originals with holographic repros and 3-D textured replicas, accelerating a process that was already underway in response to the deterioration caused by atmospheric pollution. "The age of digital reproduction has made originals increasingly obsolete," said the curator of Berlin's Havers-datter Gallery. "They will be made available to qualified academics for study."

Security was increased and museum traffic was up. It was as if by destroying great art, the "Eliminateurs" had reminded the public of its value. The damaged works were displayed in a special traveling exhibit, "Art Answers its Enemies." Reconstructions of the destroyed paintings were simultaneously exhibited to record-breaking crowds in Tokyo, London, New York, and Vancouver. By late summer, after two months without an attack, it seemed that the "Eliminateurs" were only one more of the fads that regularly rock the art world, and that the crisis was over.

Wrong on both counts.

Chapter 3

Homer was no better when I got home. I microwaved her supper along with mine, but she wouldn't eat. Homer and I had been alone together for almost nine years, since mother died. I knew from my mother that I had been named after a famous country singer by my father (whom she bitterly called the "wandering Jew"), but since we had moved from Tennessee to New York soon after my father left, I had never gotten into the music. I had never used the name. I had forgotten all about it—until I saw that picture.

That night before I went to bed, I took the LP out of the bag (even though we're strictly not supposed to) and studied the picture on the album cover. I thought of Dante: he would have grumbled if he'd seen Hank Williams. He looked Italian, like that singer that had caused so much fuss when he was pulled a few years ago, Sinatra. Except for the cowboy hat. I knew that night I would dream of the West. I leaned the album cover against the wall at the foot of my bed, and I could almost, but not quite, hear the music. A distant lonesome sound.

The next morning I had to wake up Homer again. She seemed slow on her feet, so instead of taking her out for her walk right after breakfast, I logged onto MS-MD, my HMO. I described the symptoms ("I had to wake her up and she usually wakes me up") and was given a queue number.

I only had one pickup that morning, so I took Homer with me. That was unusual—but she seemed so blue! The address was "Sunset View" on the south side of Great Kills, in the shadow of the peak. I left Homer in the lectro while I made the call.

It was a little old lady with jeweled eyeglasses. She had a couple of Grisham paperbacks and a movie, *The Sand Pebbles*. I gave Jewel 150 for the movie and explained to her that paperback books published after 20— were no-bonus. She was disappointed. Three hundred is a lot in an old folks' home where everything is free except for what's in the machines. "Why not the books?" she asked. "Grisham was pulled, I know he was. The nurse checked for me on the BAE website."

"He was deleted, that's true," I said, checking my slate and shifting into my most soothing version of info-mode. Informing the public is not only a service; it's a way of cooling them out. It's a kind of end-run around the anger you occasionally run into as a government official, particularly when there's money involved. "Grisham's books were deleted from the Library of Congress database. Which means they can no longer be downloaded into individual or institutional readers. The leftover hardcovers were picked from whatever regional libraries still kept them. But these paperbacks, some of the last to be printed, were printed on acid-rich paper. They will decay on their own." I picked up one and shook it. "It was a special arrangement. See how they powder, the pages?"

Jewel frowned and looked away. Was she a bibliophile, or was she worried about her rug? The powder was yellow on her worn maroon carpet. Then I looked at her hands, the backs of her hands, and I understood. She understood decay, but not as something that happened to the young. The books were less than twenty years old. She must have been four times that.

Homer was waiting patiently in the car. Her usually bright, beady black eyes were dull, almost gray, and her tongue was white. Her breath was terrible. I tried MS-MD again, but my queue number still hadn't come up. I logged back into the questionaire and added "white tongue" and "dull eyes" to her symptoms.

The shortest route to the D&D led over a shoulder of Great Kills Peak. I could see the perfectly symmetrical summit, which is usually wreathed in mist, so Homer and I took the serpentine up the receding benches (each a different generation of fill, with a different warm fog) to the top. On the way we passed the MS-MD Pet Annex, though I didn't notice it at the time. At 1,128 feet Great Kills is only slightly lower than the World Trade Center. You're looking down onto Todt Hill; you can see most of Manhattan and all of Brooklyn from the "New York's Cleanest" Memorial Overlook.

"This would be a great place for a restaurant," I told Homer. She nodded mournfully. "Except nobody wants to eat sitting on top of a garbage pile. But what is any city but a garbage pile, a midden? And when you think about it, what are you sitting on when you eat anyway?"

She nodded again. Even though Homer eats standing up and doesn't have to think about things like that.

I had two more pickups for the day, one of them across the bridge in Brooklyn. Both could wait until afternoon. I dropped Homer off at home, microwaved her lunch, and went to the D&D for my own. "What's in the bag, Santa?" Lou asked as he buzzed me in.

"Ever hear of Hank Williams?"

"White guy, right?" Lou's in between, like most of America. "Country and Western singer. Was he pulled? He's the kind of guy they would have made a stink about a few years ago. Like Sinatra, remember that?"

"They shoulda left Sinatra alone," said Dante, from the gloom. "He belongs to the ages."

Dante is White, or was. With his pale bald head and pale hands, he looked like a ghost in the gloom at the end of the bar. As an ex-cop (or something; I was afraid to ask) he knew better than to say Immortal.

"Williams looks like Sinatra," I said. "Or rather, looked like him."

"Well, they both belong to the ages now," said Lou. "As will we all, someday, not excluding Dante here. Have another bud on me. In memory of Hank Sinatra."

"*Frank* Sinatra," said Dante. "You forget. I remember."

"Let's see his picture," said Lou, picking up his little flashlight and shining it into my bag. "Where'd it go?"

"I—gave it back," I said. The lie jumped out of my mouth even before I remembered why I needed it. The album cover was in my room, leaning against the baseboard at the foot of my bed. Strictly against Bureau regs.

"Gave it back?" Dante asked from the darkness.

"The pickup was a false alarm."

"Bull." Dante snorted. "The guy's either pulled or not pulled."

"The album cover was empty," I said. A lie but a prescient lie, as it turned out.

"Bull. You've been to see the bootleggers."

"You're not allowed to say that, even as a joke," I reminded him. "It's a federal offense to joke about bootlegging."

"I'll say anything I fucking please," said Dante. "Begging your federal fucking pardon."

I wasn't offended. Dante's like that (or was). Anyway, I was the one who had lied, and lies don't bother me. In my job, I have to be diplomatic, so stretching or bending the truth is no big deal. I was more concerned with trying to figure out why I had taken the album cover out the the bag, and why I had never replaced it. I had never done anything of the sort before, and I had been in the Bureau since 20—.

I passed on the healthy stuff and had a grilled cheese. Comfort food. I was feeling a little strange.

My first afternoon pickup was a movie (the world is filled with movies) in Small Beach, a condo complex on the east side of the island. A woman in a wheelchair brought it to the door. It was *The Fugitive*, much on the news when it was deleted last year as it was the end, for all practical purposes, of Harrison Ford. It was at the top of a stack of videos in her lap. The wheelchair woman tried to get me to take them all; she was disappointed when I told her the rest weren't worth anything. Some of them had been pulled for over twenty years; the newest, a Western (*Bonnie and Clyde*), was almost ten years deleted.

She was more than disappointed; she was angry. Petulant is perhaps the word. She started to complain and I told her to be thankful that I was in Deletion and not Enforcement, since the penalty for keeping deleted A&E after six years is more than a fine, it's six months in a penalty shoe. Technically, of course: the rule's only enforced when there is evidence or suspicion of bootlegging. The Registry is voluntary, and no one pretends it's complete.

She was unimpressed: "Penalty shoe?" she cackled, spinning her chair all the way around as if to spite me.

I ended giving her a hundred anyway. Though she was unpleasant, she was crippled and she was alone. As far as I'm concerned, that's what discretionary is for. At bottom, ours is a people job and I'm a people person.

My second afternoon pickup was in Brooklyn, at Charlie Rose High School on 83rd and Bay Parkway. I love the drive over the bridge; it's one of the perks of having a Bureau lectro. We don't get many schools. Most of them turned in their libraries years ago, converting to servers and readers even before the "book"stores did.

A glum, girl librarian led me to a dimly-lighted storeroom. The pickup was a painting, a repro, not even dimensional, but repros are pulled along with the originals when the artist is deleted. It was a Rockwell of a whale knocking a boat out of the water from below. The kind of lurid stuff that high school kids like, or used to like, I guess. It looked pretty old.

I checked my slate: Painters, Rockwell, etc. "I don't have a Rockwell," I told the librarian. "Rockwell wasn't pulled."

"This is a different Rockwell," she said. "Rockwell Kent. He was pulled a dozen years ago."

"Over six is a problem," I said. "I'm required to tell you that . . ."

"We're not Alexandrians here!" she said, brightening for the first time. "The Registry just missed it. Hey, maybe they thought it was something by the kids."

Not very likely, I thought. Although the whale wasn't very realistic. It looked like a whale from a computer game. Too smooth.

I stuffed the repro into my bag, frame and all, and put 150 on the school's card. The deal is, if it's in the library the Board gets the money; if it's on the wall, the school.

I took the librarian's word that it had been on the wall. I wanted to give her school the money. She was about thirty, and glum again, but not bad looking, with one of those long, thoughtful faces that some people find attractive. She wore a bluebird mood sweater over a long skirt. The bluebirds were bluest on the sides of her heavy breasts, and I remember thinking they ought to have been milk-cows. I didn't often think such thoughts. I wondered if it meant I was getting over my mother's death at last. Homer would have said "about time," if Homer could talk.

The librarian was walking me to the door when I saw the record-player. In addition to knowing what it was called from Academy, I recognized it from my pickup the day before. The lid was open and big-leafed plants were growing out of the turntable part.

I stopped and said, "Excuse me?"

"Excuse me?"

I pointed at the record-player. "Where did you get that?"

"It belongs to the school," she said. "Why?"

"I just was wondering where a fellow might find one, is all."

"They're not illegal. In case you're testing me."

"I have a lot of plants."

"They're not illegal," she said again, opening the door.

"I'm a pickup artist. Deletion, not enforcement," I said. "Nobody's trying to entrap anybody. I just have a lot of plants."

She shrugged and held the door open, waiting for me to leave. The hallway was flooded with light. Through the windows I could see the Verrazzano Bridge and Staten Island beyond it. Clouds drifted off the flanks of Great Kills Peak, rising like great ghosts from the fumaroles opened by the fermenting fill.

I squeezed by her bluebirds with their angora wings. "Why don't you leave me your card," she said. "In case we come up with something else."

I don't have a lot of plants. As I drove back across the bridge to Staten Island, I wondered: Why had I told her that? And why had she mentioned the Alexandrians? They were the gang that stole art to keep it from being destroyed. Supposedly for religious reasons, not like the bootleggers, who did it for money. I say supposedly, because often the small truths we are told are only there to obscure a bigger truth.

Chapter 4

*T*he first attack on books came in September of the same year, 20—. The classics room of the New York Public Library on Fifth Avenue, and the reading room of the London Library, where Marx had patiently composed Das Kapital, were attacked simultaneously at 7:00 a.m. New York time—11:00 a.m. London time. The timing led many to assume that the attacks had been planned and coordinated from New York.

The attack was claimed by a group calling themselves Alexandrians ("after the fire, not the library").

There were no injuries, except to the classics collection in New York, which lost a first edition of Bright Lights, Big City. Responses were quick, but less than unanimous. While Pen International and the Author's Guild denounced the bombings, the Science Fiction and Fantasy Writers of America (SFWA), a shadowy organization of genre writers, fans, and hobbyists, tendered cautious support to the aims if not the practices of the bombers, venturing the opinion that perhaps it was time for the shelves to be cleared to make way for new authors. SFWA's support was seen as self-serving, since no SF or fantasy authors were included among the classics destroyed, or indeed among the classics at all.

At this time both supporters and detractors of the "Alexandrians" and "Eliminateurs" (if indeed they were separate groups) saw the attacks as merely symbolic, since publishing had ceased to be a hard copy business, and most books were files downloaded from central computers run by libraries and publishing companies.

As the year progressed, several more art museums were bombed. On November 15 the Rock and Roll Hall of Fame was destroyed in a car bomb blast that rocked Cleveland and sent a two and a half foot mini-tsunami crashing onto the stony shores of Ontario, forty miles across Lake Erie. A Toronto band, Speld Funē, wrote a rap song in honor of the event, "Johnny Be Bad."

Was it a single movement, or a loose confederation of copycats? The controversy was broadened but not resolved when the Museum of Motion Picture History in Los Angeles was bombed on the day after Thanksgiving. The next week, in an apparent copycat attack, the "Walk of the Stars" had several handprints filled with cement, including those of Marilyn Monroe and Billy Bob Thornton. "Oscar" claimed credit for both acts of cultural sabotage.

By the time the Metropolitan and the Brooklyn Museum were hit, the tenets of eliminatión, as it was called in Europe, or deletion in the USA, were a common subject of debate on the talk shows and in the press. The movement had even attracted a few sympathizers in high places, most notably (and surprisingly) the head of the NEA, Carol "Cookie" McCurdy.

Then the game turned deadly. During Christmas week, a midday blast at the Getty Museum in Los Angeles collapsed an underground parking garage, crushing a tour bus and instantly killing eighteen tourists from Stillcreek, Oregon, and their driver, Bud White, 58.

Chapter 5

Homer was no better. In fact, she was worse. When I got home from Brooklyn, I found her sleeping on my bed, which she rarely did, knowing better. I didn't smack her, though; I didn't have the heart. I fixed her dinner and, while it was microwaving, checked with MS-MD. The wait was over! I was given a voicemail number and an access code good until midnight.

I called but the line was busy.

While we ate dinner, I let the phone redial. "Be patient," I told Homer. I was speaking more to myself; patience is not a problem for most dogs, and certainly not for her. After dinner, while the phone redialed, we watched *Hollywood Squares*. It's a myth that dogs don't like to watch television. I was the one who got bored, or perhaps distracted is the word. I went into the bedroom and sat on the bed. Peering out from under his cowboy hat, Hank Williams's eyes looked beady and sad, like Homer's. On the back of the album it said he had died, but it didn't say where or when. Out West somewhere, judging by the hat.

The picture fascinated me, drew me in. It was like peering into my past. I kept seeing my father in the same hat (though in the only picture I had seen, he wore a baseball cap), his hand on my bedroom door, telling me something while my mother was yelling something from the kitchen. Then the door was closed and he was gone. I felt (I hoped? I knew?) that if I could only hear the songs on the record the picture in my mind of my father, standing in the door, would come alive, and I would remember the words he spoke as he was leaving. The words I had missed the first time around.

I pulled the record out of its cover but it was mute. Black, and grooved on both sides, and mute.

I had never before even considered breaking Bureau regs. But now I had already done it, by taking the album out of the bag. Rendering wasn't until the end of the month, which gave me almost three weeks to look at it. But look at it was all. There was no way to listen to it without a record-player, and no way a Bureau employee could buy a record-player without arousing suspicion. Even if he could find one.

The phone back-rang, and I slid the album back into the bag before answering. It wasn't a video call—I don't even have video. I did it because I was already feeling guilty.

"If you're calling about a person, press one or say person. If you're calling about a pet, press two or say pet."

It was the HMO! "Two," I said, even though I didn't (still don't!) think of Homer as a pet. After about twenty minutes of negotiating the phone tree, I finally got to a paravet SRS.

"You'll have to leave him overnight," said a warm robot voice, after hearing the symptoms. "Bring him in tomorrow morning, Wednesday, between eight and ten o'clock, Eastern standard time."

"Her," I said. "She's a her." But the line was dead.

The room looked different. I looked around and realized what was missing. The Williams. I decided to leave it in the bag where it belonged, and went into the living room to watch *Police Action* with Homer on what turned out to be our last evening together at home.

On Wednesday morning I found four pickups on my slate, a relatively busy day. But before starting anything, I took Homer straight to Great Kills.

All four sides of the steep, four-sided peak were streaked with the warm fog released by the fumaroles on the lower benches, which open under the pressure of the expanding gases in the fill. The road wound up and around, in and out of the mist, until we reached the highest bench, just above a thin layer of sweet-smelling cloud.

The MS-MD Pet Annex was a small concrete block building with a single glass door and no windows, even though it had, through a keyhole slot in the clouds, the best view on Staten Island.

I buzzed and the nurse came to the door with a little device like a kazoo that allowed her to talk through the glass. I suppose it was supposed to seem more personal than a speakerphone.

"I have an appointment," I shouted through the glass. I shouted my access number, and Homer's SDS. She nodded and buzzed us in. "This is only for a day or so," I reminded Homer, dismayed by her mournful look. "They are going to run a few tests. Right, Mrs. Quilvárres?"

It always helps when you use people's names. You can learn more from reading name tags than books.

"That's all up to the Vet Team," she said, unclipping my line and putting Homer on hers. "What coverage did you say you had?"

I always liked that question, whether asked of Homer or me, since the answer invariably improves the service. "MS, Federal. BAE. Homer is attached as a rider."

"Yes, sir." She swiped my cashcard for the copayment. "Would you like to see his room?"

"Her," I said. "Thanks, but I have to go to work." I could hear wild barking from the back of the building.

The nurse locked me out and Homer looked back at me, dragging her big feet on the smooth, tiled floor as the nurse led her away.

"Back soon!" I mouthed through the glass, wishing I had a kazoo. "Promise!"

The first pickup of the day was an anthology of sea poetry on Hylan Boulevard. It was a fat coffee table book, illustrated, and the fat woman who owned it was surly when I explained that she couldn't collect for each individual poet. She wanted money for the illustrators, too. One of them was the same Rockwell I had picked up at Charlie Rose High the day before, from the glum librarian with the bluebird sweater and the milk-cow breasts.

"This one, this one, and this one," said the Fat Lady, citing me the dates when each poet had appeared on the list. She had obviously spent a lot of time on the Bureau's website calculating her bonuses, but little time examining the rules and restrictions. I patiently (or so it seemed to me) explained that once half the sea poets have been pulled, the book hits the Registry as one unit.

"The reward stays the same but the penalties are waived," I said as I swiped her card for 150. The word *reward* is one we learn to use in training; it supposedly calms recalcitrant clients. I didn't point out that the penalties are routinely waived, except in cases of deliberate retention.

"Isn't there a statute of limitations or something?" she asked. Then she slammed the door before I could figure out, or even ask, what she meant.

Not that I cared. It was almost noon. I had another take-out within a mile of Hylan—a Stephen King. We get at least one of those a week; it makes you wonder how many old hardcovers or pre-acid paperbacks are still around, in attics and closets around the country. And every one worthless, of course, since they are over six years old.

Neverthless it's up to me to explain the rules to the clients, who can read but won't.

"What's in the bag, Santa?" asked Lou, as he cracked an egg into my cup. I showed him, or rather, opened the bag and let him see.

"I thought you took Frank Williams back," he said.

"Hank," said Dante, from the darkness.

"Another screwup," I said. I was amazed at how quickly

each new lie appeared on my lips. "You know the Bureau. Do it, then do it again."

"Bullshit," said Dante. When he spoke I could see him in the gloom; when he was silent, he was invisible, almost. "Don't you know there's a counter on that bag. You can't be taking stuff in and out. And what's the point, without a record-player."

None of Dante's questions were questions. None required answers. They made me nervous anyway. Could he be an ex-cop working for Enforcement? I wondered. He knew too much about the Bureau, and about me as well. I imagined he knew more about what I was up to than I did. And what's worse, it was true, he did.

Lou came to the rescue. That's a bartender's job. "Record-players aren't all that rare," he said. "People buy them to make into planters. 'Course, not in stores, since there aren't any new ones."

"Flee markets?" I asked. Flee markets were unregulated since they straddled, or pretended to straddle, state lines.

Lou shook his head. "They're not that legal. Then there's always the misdemeanor clubs where they'll play anything for you."

"I thought they were shut down."

Dante snorted. "Haven't you ever heard of Brooklyn."

Lou pointed at my glass. "Have another egg?"

The afternoon was as uneventful as the morning: a Brooklyn Dodgers picture book in a run-down old folks' home on the high side of Victory Boulevard, and a Steve Earle CD. Country music was always big on Staten Island. This one was from a box that a pimply kid had inherited from his grandfather. How it got into our database, I don't know. Pimples was clearly more interested in the 150 than the law. That's often the case. One-fifty to a kid is a lot of money.

Maybe I'm a pushover. Maybe I was getting burned out and didn't know it.

The house seemed empty. I couldn't face the microwave, so I went out for Chinese. It wasn't until I got home that I remembered to check my messages. There was nothing from the HMO, which was good, I suppose. But there was a strange message in a rasping voice with a strange accent, giving me the address of a misdemeanor club in Brooklyn, and a password: *Lucky dog*.

Chapter 6

World political and religious leaders, backed by their various national and international security organizations, vowed to hunt down and punish the terrorists responsible for the deaths in the Getty garage. The first break came less than a month after the tragedy. Even as the Pope was denouncing "those who would defile the legacy of the ages," his Swiss Guard captured two men and a woman setting a firebomb in the gallery of the New Vatican in Vegas. While the Pope was silent and even forgiving, the Swiss Guard (unconstrained by the US's elaborate criminal-protection laws) began a rigorous interrogation in the New Vatican's extensive basements.

Confessions quickly followed, leading to eleven arrests in Los Angeles, Vegas, and New York. Most of those arrested were obscure artists, writers, and "wannabees," motivated as much by envy as ideology (though envy itself is considered by some to be an ideology). But among them was screen star Damaris Dolores, known in her later films simply as Damaris, at one time the third-highest-paid female film star in Hollywood, the winner of one Academy Award (Best Supporting Actress, *Off The Shoulder*) and four times a nominee, who was arrested as she was leaving her walled Beverly Hills compound for an animal rights benefit in nearby North Hollywood.

Los Angeles won the jurisdictional toss, and in spite of the fact that the high casualties were suspected to be a result of shoddy construction (later confirmed in a civil litigation) and illegal van design *(also confirmed to the tune of eighteen million), Los Ange-les County District Attorney Lourdes Fonda declared her intention not to petition the president for a death penalty exemption.*

Chapter 7

One-eighty-two Bay Parkway was a three-story frame house over a concrete block basement with painted windows. A couple of Black guys hung around outside, flanking the door. They eyed me suspiciously until I said, "Lucky dog." They both nodded in weird unison, and continued to eye me suspiciously as I went down three steps and knocked. There was a time when anyone who wasn't entirely White was considered Black, but that was in my childhood. Nowadays, most people are in-between like myself. Black as well as White is mostly attitude. Of course, these two were probably paid to look menacing.

The door opened and I paid my five and slipped in. It was only then, as the door clicked shut behind me, that I considered what I was doing. It was like a compulsion, done out of the eyesight of thought. I had taken precautions, of course. I was wearing a knit hat. I had changed out of my sky blue, one-stripe Bureau pants, and I was carrying the Hank Williams album in a shopping bag so it looked like anything. Or nothing.

I had read about the misdemeanor clubs, but this was my first time inside one. They had been popular right after BAE was chartered. Now it seemed like nobody cared. Enforcement still raided one or two a month, nationwide, just to keep them in the news. Surely, I thought, I can get away with this one thing, this one time. Hear the record and go home and no one the wiser.

The club was about half filled with people watching TV and listening to music. A few Blacks, a few Whites, but most intermediates like myself, and mostly bored.

Everyone sat at his or her own table. The music was jazz, as far as I could tell. I saw somebody give the bartender a five and a CD. Was that the drill? I had come too far to turn back. The bartender took my five but he gave me a blank look when I pulled the Williams out of the shopping bag and set it on the bar. "No wax," he said. "Only on Mondays."

He slid me a bud instead of giving me the five back, and I slid the record album back into the shopping bag, feeling strangely relieved, even exhilarated. I had dared and failed. I had been saved in spite of myself. By Monday the album would be at Worth Street and my life would be back to normal.

There were no stools at the bar, so I took my bud to a table, figuring to drink it and go home. There was a TV in each corner, high on the wall, playing without sound. They were showing an old sitcom that had long been pulled. It showed a bunch of people on an island, arguing. They lived in small tents. I found the whole scene amusing. If it hadn't been pulled, if it wasn't forbidden fruit, would anyone still be watching?

Not that anyone was. Most of the customers were staring into their buds as if they were little, long-necked oracles. Perhaps they were listening to the music. Still jazz; you can tell by the instrumentation. I finished my bud and stood up, ready to go, just as the door opened. Somebody on the TV was trying to break a coconut with a woman's high-heeled shoe.

I realized what was strange about the voice on my machine when I saw the librarian walk in. It had been a woman's voice disguised as a man's. Hers. She was wearing the same bluebird sweater and a much shorter skirt.

I sat back down. She pretended to be surprised to see me. She sat down across from me. The bluebirds on her breasts were very dim. She seemed nervous.

I decided to pretend I didn't know it was her voice on my machine. "Imagine seeing you here," I said. "Can I buy you a bud?"

She said yes, but only one.

I brought it from the bar. "I don't even know your name," I said as I placed the bottle in front of her.

"Henry," she said. "Short for Henrietta."

I told her my name was Hank, surprising myself. It was the first time I had used that name since Mother had died, and that was . . .

"Then we have the same name," she said.

"We do?"

"Hank is short for Henry, I think," she said. "Anyway, I really admire what you do."

"You what? You do?"

"The Bureau," she said. "I mean, the tree of art, unless pruned, will stop bearing fruit."

"We're not just art," I said. "We do music, literature and movies. No fruit."

"I know," she said. "It's a metaphor."

"We don't do metaphors either," I said. Then added: "It's a joke."

There was an awkward silence. We both took a sip of bud. On the TV, they were still trying to break the coconut. Now they were hitting it with the butt of a gun—an ancient Webley .38 revolver.

"It must be a dangerous job," she said. "I mean, with the Alexandrians and bootleggers and everything."

"I don't get involved with all that," I replied. "I'm not in Enforcement. And under the law I am required to remind you that . . ."

"We're in a misdemeanor club," she said. "We can talk about anything, almost. Even bootleggers."

I shrugged. I wasn't so sure. "I'm just a pickup artist," I said.

"A take what?"

"Pickup artist is the name Enforcement gives us. I think they meant it as an insult. Because we don't arrest anybody."

"You should be proud of that," she said.

I wasn't so sure. "Why?"

There was another awkward silence. "So why are you here?" she asked, in a whisper. "What's in the bag?"

"Nothing," I said. I had forgotten it. I slid it under the table. "I got the idea from you."

Henry looked alarmed, and I added quickly: "From your school, I mean. I'm looking for a record-player. To make into a planter. I have a lot of plants. Remember?"

"A turntable?"

"A turntable is just a component," I said. "A record-player is the whole thing in one. The knobs are on the front of the box."

"You have a lot of plants," she said. I could tell she didn't believe me. She looked at the shopping bag again, then looked around the club, but didn't see whatever—or who-ever—she was looking for. We both looked back up at the TV. A guy in a funny hat was holding the coconut in front of his chest, while a girl pointed the gun at it. "Which one is Gilligan?" I asked.

"Gilligan is the girl," Henry said.

Gilligan was just about to pull the trigger when the door opened and a small man in a cowboy hat came into the club. I noticed that he didn't have to pay. I tried to remember if Henry had paid.

She waved at him and he came and stood by our table. I could barely see a dark face under the brim of the cowboy hat.

"Hank, meet Cowboy Bob," she said. "Bob can get you just about anything you care to need. Like a record-player."

Henry got up. Bob sat down.

"It's for a planter," I said.

"Let me see in the bag," Bob said. "They come in different speeds. I have to make a match."

I handed him the shopping bag and he peered in and nod-ded, reminding me, for a moment, of Lou. "Thirty-three and one-third. Difficult but easy if you know what I mean. Bring it here, tomorrow night, same time."

Then he got up and was gone. "Bring what?" I asked, too late.

Henry sat down with two buds. "My turn to buy," she said. The bluebirds were back on her breasts. They flew slowly across from left to right. I noticed that she had tiny, nice hands. Librarian hands, I guess.

"We didn't talk about the price," I said.

"If I know Bob, you'll be pleased," said Henry. Then she smiled for the first time: "And I know Bob."

For myself, I wished I didn't. On the TV they were trying to set up a tent. Everything they tried to do went wrong. I knew the feeling. My exhilaration was gone. I had gotten entangled in something illegal, and I knew that I was going to play it on out.

Maybe it would be okay. Tomorrow was Friday. I would keep the album for an extra day. Worth Street would never know. Then I would turn it in and turn the record-player into a planter. It would work out. I didn't even care about hearing the record anymore, the lonesome songs. The compulsion would be gone, and with it the danger.

Meanwhile, there was the girl, Henry. I decided to ask her to dance. I bought two more buds, but when I turned to carry them to "our" tiny round table, I saw that Henry was already gone.

I drank them both myself, at the bar.

Chapter 8

*A*t their arraignment, each for nineteen counts of murder in the first degree and two counts of aggravated intentional terrorist assault (there were two simultaneous explosions), the "Getty 11" made no statements and refused legal assistance. The judge announced plans to appoint counsel and entered a plea of "not guilty" for each of the defendants, as required by law. She then granted bail (as required under California's Celebrity Code) to Damaris, releasing her on her own recognizance as a low-risk defendant who would have "no place to hide." The ten others were denied bail and remanded to Los Angeles County Jail.

Damaris refused bail, in solidarity with her codefendants. "Ours is a war against Celebrity itself," she said in a press conference on the steps of the jail after she was ejected. The resulting media furor (Damaris, in her orange jumpsuit, was on the covers of all four tabloids for the first time in twelve years) resulted in a temporary federal injunction solicited by the survivors and friends of the victims, constituting themselves legally as The Loved Ones, Inc., "reminding the court" (as their attorneys put it) of the equal coverage guaranteed under the Victims' Rights Amendment to the Constitution.

The judge's eviction order was rescinded and Damaris was readmitted to the Los Angeles County Jail, though separated from her codefendants and confined in the Celebrity wing. Jury selection began, and the press and the world prepared for the first Celebrity trial in which the crime was a war on Fame itself.

Chapter 9

I woke up at home alone.

It was bleak without Homer.

It was incredibly, astonishingly, awesomely lonely.

I lay with my eyes closed, listening to my slate beep, listening to the emptiness of the big old house I had inherited from my father via my mother. Without Homer, it was only a house. Less than a house: just a bunch of rooms and halls stitched together by silence.

I was alone except for Hank Williams, who was propped against the wall across from my bed. He looked a lot like Cowboy Bob in his cowboy hat, getting into his lectro. But it would have been a gas-o-line car in those days. Probably a Cadillac. *Where was he going? What was he trying to tell me?*

Tonight I would find out. This morning the scheme didn't look so bad. I would come home and play the record once, then put it back into the Bureau bag for rendering on Friday, and turn the record-player into a planter, and all would be well again. I could almost hear the song in my mind, a whining sound, like a car going away.

I got up and checked my slate. I only had three pick-ups. Things at the Bureau were slow, and getting slower—either because deletions (and therefore pick-ups) were off, or people were more civic-minded (bringing them in voluntarily). Not that it mattered to me; I got paid the same either way.

I started to drop the Williams album into my bag, and then thought better of it. I would only have to take it out again tonight. There was a rumor that everything that went in or out of a Bureau bag was monitored by an invisible electrical plasma membrane connected by satellite to Worth Street. I didn't pay attention to Academy rumors even while I was at Academy, much less after. But why take a chance? I left the album propped against the wall and hit the road.

Great Kills was wreathed in odoriferous mist. Although I had been told the tests might take several days, I called the Pet Annex. I wanted Homer to know, somehow, that I was thinking about her. All I got was a busy signal.

My first pickup was on Front Street, down in the old St. George section. It was a young couple who worked on Wall Street and commuted on the ferry. They had bought the house six months before (they explained this very carefully) and had been too busy to notice the small library of hardcover books in the basement bathroom. They had been so busy fixing up the house, choosing colors and so forth that they hadn't checked the authors against the website—even though this is, of course, required by law. You can't always get to everything right away. You understand . . . ?

"I understand," I said. I even nodded. I wasn't looking to bust anybody. Diplomacy, that's what my job is all about. Was all about. Is all about.

"So when we heard that Grisham had been deleted, we called," she said. They were of course, "also interested in the bonus."

I shook my head. Discretionary was, as I saw it, for people who needed it. "The bonus is the feeling of doing your civic duty," I said. "After the first year, the bonus kicks out and the penalty kicks in."

"Penalty?"

I let the word hang in the air for a few moments. Looking back from here, I can see that my own criminality, in thought as well as deed, made me more than willing to taunt them. Perhaps that is why there is such a thin line between police and criminals; they (we?) both operate in the same shadowy half world.

"The penalties for withholding are well known," I said finally. "That's all on the Bureau's site, too. I'm sure you looked it up."

"We don't have time to look up everything," said the man. "That stuff's worth money, you know."

I reminded them that it was illegal to even suggest bootlegging, put the two books in my bag and left. Did I mention that they had a dog? An unpleasant little yapping item.

It was almost lunchtime. I had successfully killed the morning. I tried the Pet Annex and got another busy signal. Although it wasn't on my way to the D&D, I drove up the square shoulder of the mountain. The Pet Annex was above the three hundred meter line, and wreathed in clouds. I drove by it but all I could see was the sign, the fence, and a shadow that might have been the building.

I hit redial on the way down, and this time I got an answer: "Pet Annex, your caring Care Center."

I grabbed for the phone and hit speaker at the same time, almost swerving off the narrow road. "Hello! Patient Information please."

"Name and number?"

"Yes, yes, yes . . ." I gave them my name and number.

"I'll be glad to connect you. Please hold."

So there I was, on hold. Through the first gate, as it were. I let the hold music play as I drove down the mountain to the D&D. Inside, I set my phone on the bar beside my bud, turned way down so only I could hear the hold music.

"How was it," said Dante from his dark corner.

"How was what?"

"The misdemeanor club."

"I'm a federal employee, I can't go to a misdemeanor club," I said. I thought that was pretty clever, avoiding a lie by telling the truth. But Dante just snorted into his bud.

"How's Hank Williams?" asked Lou.

"In the bag," I said. Hoping he wouldn't look. To change the subject I told him my dog was in the hospital, and I was waiting for the "doctor" to call. I nodded toward the phone on the bar. Lou wiped around it sympathetically. I lingered over my lunch, waiting to hear a tiny voice instead of tiny music. But there was nothing.

I had two afternoon pickups. The first was in "Sunset Corridors," a franchise old folks' home in the High Clove section of Todt Hill. It looked classy from the outside but the smell inside was low and awful. The old man whose name was on the slate wore a string tie over a soup-stained shirt. He was surprised to see me. The pickup was a CD box set—a long pulled and long forgotten crooner named George Jones, who had been called in by what we call an *anon*.

Stringtie had tears, or what appeared to be tears, in his eyes as I dropped the CDs into my bag. Meanwhile, an old woman across the day room was grinning. A revenge pickup. I couldn't help seeing myself in the old man she had turned in. He had not been bootlegging, although under the law it was no different. With the delicious knowledge that I was disappointing the informant, I not only didn't fine him, but gave him the discretionary bonus.

Back in my car, I was still on hold. But only for a moment. As I was pulling off through the drifting leaves, I heard a tiny voice: "Mr. Shapiro?"

"Yes! That's me. Pet Annex? Patient Information?"

"You have to speak to a Grief Counselor first."

"A what? What's going on?!"

"Procedure. You have a Q number before you can access a Grief Counselor."

"I don't want a Grief Counselor!"

"Please hold for your Q number."

To hell with that! I thought, and hung up.

My last pickup was a hardcover volume of *Best American Short Stories, 2014*. The bounty is not good on anthologies until half of the authors have been pulled, and this one was only down seven out of nineteen. But I didn't care. I couldn't get my mind off Homer. I ran through my routine like a zombie: smile, sign off, swipe cards, pay money, stash loot into the bag and walk out into the late afternoon sun—never dreaming that this would be, if not the last pickup of my career, the last on Staten Island—and the last with the Bureau as I knew it.

All I knew then was that I had successfully killed the afternoon. I headed for home for supper and to kill a couple more hours. There were two messages. A gruff voice which I recognized as Henry's, disguised, said, "The word tonight is tender loin." The other was an HMO operator with my Q number for Grief Counseling—Q7865-78.

Grief Counseling? I still didn't like the sound of it. But I had to find out something. I dialed the MS-MD, punched in the number . . . and was put back on hold. The music was that generic stuff that truly *is* immortal because it never had a composer.

It was time for supper but I had lost my appetite. The house seemed cold and empty. I decided to head to Brooklyn a little early. Anything beat hanging around the house waiting for the hold music to stop again. I left, remembering at the last minute to bring the Williams album with me.

The call came through on the bridge. Oddly enough it happened just as the clouds were clearing, and I could see, if only for a moment, and only in my rearview mirror, the perfectly symmetrical summit of Great Kills shining in the sun's last light; and a little block near the top that might have been the Pet Annex itself. "Mr. Shapiro?"

"Yes! Pet Annex? I want Patient Information, please!"

"You have to go through Grief. Do you have a counselor?"

"I don't want a counselor. I want Patient Information."

"Then one will be assigned. Please hold while I connect you."

"I don't want a fucking counselor." But I was on hold again. A lectro honked behind me, then another, and I realized I had slowed almost to a stop. I sped up and cut over to the slow lane.

"Grief. Hal here. Get over it."

"Hello? Get over what? Has something happened to Homer?"

"It's a joke. Just kidding. Name's Hal, as in 'How can I help?' And who the hell's Homer?"

"Homer is my dog," I said. "A patient at Pet Annex. I don't need counseling. I need Patient Information."

"Man's best friend," said Hal. "Next to the telephone, of course. Joke. Is this Shapiro? Q7865-78?"

"Yes, and I don't fucking need counseling. I need Patient Information."

"That's okay," said Hal. "I'm here if you need me. You have to go through me when there's a serious illness involved. It's for your protection, okay?"

"What serious illness?"

"Confidential! I can't reveal that. But now that we've talked I can sign off on you and give you a Q number for Patient Information. Okay?"

"Okay."

"Write this down! It's Q . . . uh . . . whoa!"

"Whoa what?"

"Shapiro, they've got you shunted directly to ONC."

"ONC?"

"Oncology Choices. Look man, maybe we *do* need to talk. Sometimes the hardest thing is finding somebody who cares."

"Cares about what? What's going on?"

"Don't freak out!" said Hal. "Be cool. That's the main thing. Let me put you on hold while I connect you with ONC."

"No . . ."

But it was too late. I was on hold again. I was at the top of the bridge, heading down. It was rush hour and the bridge was streaming with lectros and cars, all heading west, out of Brooklyn, toward the setting sun. I was one of the few going east.

I was only on hold for a moment. "You have reached Pet Annex, Oncology Choices Department. Our offices are open, as required by law, from eight to five. Please call in the morning after eight A.M. please."

"One please would be enough," I muttered, and hung up. The phone was dead. No music, no information, no nothing.

Curiously, I was relieved, or at least I thought I was relieved, as I drove on down, off the ramp, into the lights of Brooklyn, scattered, low, like fallen stars. There was nothing I could do until morning.

Chapter 10

A Celebrity trial is best conducted by Celebrities. The prosecution of the "Getty 11" was led by Assistant DA Byron Addison Wilson, great-grandson of the most famous (and most notorious) of the Beach Boys. The defense team, appointed by the judge over the defendants' protests, was led by Lorraine Grisham Kunstler, great-great-granddaughter of the twentieth-century activist/attorney and granddaughter of a popular novelist of the 19—s. The other defense attorneys were chosen by lot from a three-county pool.

The judge was (she let it be discovered) the illegitimate granddaughter of Judge Lance Ito.

Damaris appeared in court every day in full makeup and a Chanel suit, under special order from Judge Levy-Gomez-Ito, who was afraid that trying a Movie Star in a jumpsuit would be prejudicial and might constitute grounds for appeal or even reversal. Damaris was therefore taken from her cell to a wardrobe trailer every morning on her way to the courtroom, which meant that she had to awaken an hour earlier than her ten codefendants.

These were a mixed and, it must be said, a not very colorful lot. Though their names have long since been erased under the Identity Termination Supplement to the Standardized Capital Punishment Code, it can be said that they were six men and four women and included a landscape architect, a high school band teacher, and two science fiction writers. Several had tenuous ties to the film industry. Two were married, but not to each other. Two were gay. One had a mem-

orable laugh, and another was congenitally morose. All were in between racially and culturally except for two Whites, one Black, and one self-identified Hispanic. All spoke English. "It would be difficult," said Variety, *which led the pool in covering the trial, "to imagine a more significant social movement started by a less promising group, unless one were to examine the early history of rock 'n' roll."*

The jurors were entirely anonymous and totally forgettable. Mostly retired municipal employees. Mostly women, with three men.

Of the Loved Ones, Inc., the less said the better. Unremarkable then, they are unremembered now. The judge's order that every story about the defendants had to be balanced by a story about the victims or The Loved Ones, Inc., had no practical effect, since Damaris was exempt from that restriction as a Movie Star under the Celebrity Access provisions of California's controversial Proposition 112.

Damaris was on three tabloids the second week, and four again the third.

Chapter 11

T ender loin."

The same two Black guys gave me the same hard look at the door. The same unfriendly non-Lou bartender was serving the same buds. The same *Gilligan's Island* was playing on the TV monitors in the ceiling corners, soundlessly as ever.

There was no sign of Cowboy Bob, if that was indeed his name, or Henry, if indeed that was hers. But then, I was early. I stashed the Williams album under a table and sat down to wait for nine o'clock. The "jukebox" was playing Buck Owens and John Coltrane, both of whom I recognized from Academy, since they had been pulled at the height of their popularity and were often bootlegged. I tried not to think about Homer. I had another bud.

At nine sharp the door swung inward and in walked Henry, bluebird sweater and all.

She acted surprised to see me. "Weren't you supposed to change out of those pants?"

I looked down and realized I was wearing my one-stripe, sky blue Bureau pants. "I should go," I said. "This whole thing was a bad idea."

"It's only a misdemeanor."

"Not for me. Not for us."

Instead of answering she picked up my bud and finished it. "I think we should dance while we're waiting," she said, standing up. "It looks less suspicious. What's this?"

She pointed at the Williams album in its shopping bag under the table. This time I told her.

"You're a bootlegger? I knew it." I was about to

deny it, and warn her, but she slipped so easily into my arms that I let it go for the moment. It was as if we danced together every night. I had in fact never danced with her, or any girl, or anyone before, except my mother. But I did pretty good. She seemed to think so, anyway. Her breasts were soft and big and the bluebirds were coming out, first one and then another. Her hands was small in mine.

I was getting ready to tell her that it was against the law to even joke about bootleggers when I felt something cold on the back of my neck. Night air. I turned and saw Bob, coming in the door in his cowboy hat. Henry and I stopped dancing and she stepped out of my arms; her bluebirds started to fade.

Bob was holding the album when I got to the table.

"I just want to listen to it once," I explained. "Then it goes back to—where it came from."

"Whatever," he said. He slipped the black record in and out of the album cover. It made a faint whispery sound. "I can let you have the record-player for a hundred."

That was cheaper than I had expected. I gave him five twenties, folded, under the table. As if to ridicule my caution, he counted it on the table. Meanwhile Henry, who had disappeared, came back with two buds. Was the second one mine or Bob's?

Bob's. He took a drink with one hand while he refolded the money and slipped it into a pocket with the other. Then he pulled out a thumb-blank, pressed his right thumb against it and handed it to me.

"There's a van across the street. It says 'Bob' on the side. The player's in the back, by the door. You've got a lectro to put it in?"

I nodded and stood up. Bob and I both reached for the album at the same time.

Bob won. "I'll keep this till you come back with the blank. That way I know you won't run off with my van."

It was my turn to say "Whatever." The Black guys glared

as I went outside. The cool autumn air cut through the haze of the buds and I realized I was a little drunker than I wanted to be. I wished I was home. I could hear sirens in the distance.

The van was blue and orange, a Gilette; INDIAN BOB'S was painted on the side. Indian Bob's what? And so much for the cowboy story. Through the little window in the back I could see a few framed paintings, stacked upright, a rolled up rug, and a record-player. I pressed the thumb-blank into the key panel on the rear door and it sprang open.

The record-player was the size of a small suitcase, complete with handle. As I picked it up and closed the van door, a lectro cruised by slowly with its lights off. It was the same color as mine: a sky blue Toshiba. I could see four men inside, two in the front and two in the back.

All four were watching me, even the driver.

Enforcement? Was I being followed? Even if I wasn't, my sky-blue, one-stripe pants gave me away as a Bureau employee. I couldn't put the record-player into my lectro—and I certainly couldn't let them see me carry it into the misdemeanor club.

Trying to look casual, I carried the record-player down the sidewalk like a suitcase until the lectro went around the corner.

Then I ran across the street to the club.

The two Black guys glared at me but swung the door open and closed it behind me. Henry and Bob were sitting at the table, both sipping buds. The album was underneath, between them, in its shopping bag where I had left it.

I started across the dance floor. Suddenly I felt something cold on the back of my neck. Night air again. The door swung wide and two men wearing ski masks burst into the room.

One held a Woodpecker and the other a Carillon. I knew both guns. We study weapons at Academy, before getting assigned to either Deletion or Enforcement.

The lights went down and the music stopped, simultaneously. The room was filled with shrieks and screams. Something smashed into the record-player and knocked it out of my arms. I saw Henry stand and Bob kneel. I heard the *buddha buddha buddha* of the Carillon, and a rattling that sounded like a dog dragging a chain across a porch.

Then *tak-tak-tak!* The Woodpecker.

I ran for the table but it was knocked over, and splintered—the unrifled Carillon fires dum-dum "tumblers." My album was gone. Where was Bob?

Then I saw him running for the bar, holding my album in one hand and his bud in the other.

"Come on!" Henry was pulling at my arm. I stumbled over the record-player and bent down to pick it up.

Buddha buddha buddha.

The record-player was smashed, broken open like a square egg. Wire and glass fell out when I tried to pick it up. "Come on!" said Henry, but where was Bob? Where was the Hank Williams album? Had I been caught in a Bureau raid? But the Bureau never used Carillons; they were illegal. And certainly not in a misdemeanor club where the worst penalty was supposedly a summons.

Tak-tak-tak!

I stood up and, even though I wasn't running, hit something hard and fell. A table edge? "Come on," Henry yelled. She was pulling at me, dragging me into a crowd of people who squeezed out a side door, into the cool night air. "Where's your lectro?"

I pointed down the street. She took off running and I tried to follow but my legs seemed to want to go in two different directions at once.

Tak-tak-tak! The shots were all behind me, inside the building, far away.

My one-stripe, sky blue pants were all wet. I was embarrassed and then I saw that it was blood and I sat down in the leaves, on the curb, alarmed. Leaves were sticking to me.

Henry was gone. There was Bob's Gilette van, pulling out. I tried to yell but I couldn't get my breath and besides, I was moving again, through the leaves. Walking? Henry was back, pulling my hand. She pressed it against a key pad and the door of my lectro sprung open, knocking me back down into the leaves.

Buddha buddha buddha.

The guns were outside again.

Henry was pulling at me again. The leaves were sticky with blood, messing me up. Messing up the lectro. In the distance I could hear sirens, getting closer.

"Come on!" said Henry.

"I'm doing the best I can," I said, and that's the best I could do; and that's the last thing I remember of my old life, the one that was torn from me like the leaves are torn from the trees. Which leaf goes with which tree? And does it matter anymore?

Chapter 12

*T*he trial began with a ruling by Judge Ito-Gomez-Levy that only the forensic and legal issues of the actual blast and the resultant deaths would be addressed, and that she would allow no testimony about the motivations or aims of the group. The Alexandrians (as they came to be called) responded by firing their attorneys and making Damaris their spokesperson and legal representative. The judge's ensuing contempt citation had no effect, since they were all on trial for their lives anyway and "fully expected to be convicted" (Variety).

It was, therefore, Damaris who stunned the world by changing the collective plea to guilty, and claiming for the Alexandrians ("named for the fire, not the library") responsibility not only for the Getty tragedy but for every bombing and sabotage by the "deletion" or Alexandrian movement in the past eighteen months—this even though it would have been a logistical impossibility. Before she was silenced by the judge, Damaris said the aim had been, and still was, to "wake up the world to the glut of art and information."

The press went wild. Was she shielding a movement, or using the trial to build one? Judge Gomez-Ito-Levy (she rotated the names so as not to privilege any particular ancestor) responded by dismissing the jury, as they were no longer required for the registration and administration of a guilty plea. This prompted a flurry of motions and appeals from the jurors and their attorneys which resulted in the reinstatement of the jurors as international observers, even though the *plea change was allowed to stand, and the jurors were allowed to deliver the judge's verdict, in a reversal of the usual procedure.*

The verdict itself was never in doubt. The jury foreman opened the envelope at 4:47 p.m. Pacific time on April 21, 20—. All eleven were found guilty of murder in the first degree, aggravated assault, and conspiracy to destroy private property. The Loved Ones, Inc., applauded. The Alexandrians held hands in stony silence. The judge delayed sentencing for one month in order to accommodate a petition by the jurors asking that their observer role be extended to the penalty phase since they all had book and television deals, and therefore a "substantial material interest" in the sentencing.

Chapter 13

Something was wrong. I didn't have to pee. Usually when I wake up, I have to pee first thing.

My leg felt funny. I lifted up the sheet and looked under it. My sky blue, one-stripe Bureau pants were gone—and so was the blood I remembered. Instead, there was a *thing* on my left thigh, halfway between my knee and my underpants. It looked like a pink pancake.

It was oddly warm, almost hot. Odder still, even though I had never seen one, I knew exactly what it was. It was a Cupper™, manufactured by Olean under license from Buenas Noticias Ltd. Intnl. It was the institutional-strength model, which could only be applied or removed by a licensed physician. It was not to be used to treat cancer or any proliferating tissue diseases. I was not to use alcohol or prescription drugs while it was in place. I was not to drive or operate heavy machinery. I was to call my physician if it got noticeably bigger or smaller.

I knew all that, but how? Had I been told, or was the Cupper™ one of those new medicines that released info-nanos into the bloodstream? It seemed that that knowledge itself would be part of the info. I couldn't remember a doctor of any kind. I didn't know what was under the Cupper™ but I assumed a bullet hole. I assumed I had been shot in the leg. I remembered the blood, the blow. There had been a raid . . . or had there? Enforcement didn't raid misdemeanor clubs . . . or use bullets.

Or did they? I almost sat up, but it's hard to sit up without bending your legs. Instead I just looked around.

I was in a strange apartment, which I assumed was Henry's. Had I been told that, too? Or was it just that the furnishings, the decor, had a slightly prim "librarian" look? Then I saw a bluebird bra hanging out of a half-open dresser drawer—the cup size suggested Henry.

I felt for a bullet hole in the back of my leg, but there was nothing. No hole, no Cupper™. If a bullet had gone in—and I was pretty sure it had—it hadn't come out. That was okay with me. I closed my eyes and went back to sleep.

When I woke up again it was afternoon. I could tell by the light. I still didn't have to pee. My left leg was stiff; I couldn't bend it. The Cupper™ was warm to the touch, hotter than my skin. The other leg seemed okay. I still had my "private parts." I counted my fingers. I patted my cheeks. I ran my tongue around my teeth. So far, so good.

I was damned lucky, wasn't I!?

I wasn't feeling particularly lucky.

I sat up, edging my leg off the bed. I could see a sunny kitchen through a door beyond the bureau with the bra. I looked around for my pants. Gone. So were my shoes and socks. So was my phone, and something else was missing . . .

The Williams. The album! I closed my eyes and remembered the door opening, the masked men . . . and Bob with the album.

Now I knew why I wasn't feeling lucky. If it was gone, everything was gone: my job. My house. My retirement. My life.

I was already on my feet, hopping on my right leg, before the pain hit. I ignored it and hopped through the door, into the tiny kitchen. There was my phone on the metal-topped table. There were my shoes and socks on a chair. There were my one-stripe, sky blue pants on the chair, stiff with blood. It was amazing how stiff my blood became, once it was out of my body. And cold.

But no album, no Williams!

I groaned and sat down, slowly, keeping my leg straight.

There was a window over the sink and through it, through a narrow air shaft, I could see the long strand of the bridge, and beyond it—nothing. Staten Island was wrapped in fog. That meant it was late afternoon.

No album meant I was no longer a pickup artist. I was a bootlegger, a criminal, a has-been.

Then I saw the note on the table, under my phone:

Shapiro:
We couldn't take you to a hospital. You have Bob to thank. You have to stay off your feet for a few days. I'll be home after school. Don't call me at school!
—Henrietta

Bob to thank for what? Did that mean he had saved the album for me? I could only hope so. Meanwhile, I had no intention of calling Henry at school. I had other things to worry about. The missing album had reawakened all my anxieties: like my job, my lectro, and my dog. Homer. Had I really forgotten Homer?

But first things first. I called in sick, which simply meant calling Worth Street and punching in 7425 or saying "sick." That gave me until Monday.

Then I searched recent incoming and redialed the number I had gotten on the bridge the night before. The phone rang once.

"Pet Annex, Oncology Choices Department. How may I direct your call?"

"I don't know," I said. "I wanted Patient Information, but I got shunted here last night. I'm just trying to get . . ."

"May I have your patient ID number, please?"

That part was easy.

"Please hold for the next available doctor . . ."

A doctor? "I just want—"

But it was too late. The hold music was already playing, distant and patient in my ear. I set the phone down and looked for something to eat. All I could find in the refrigerator was yogurt; in the pantry, peanut butter. I wasn't hungry anyway.

And I could hardly believe I still didn't have to pee!

Then I heard my name. I grabbed up the phone. "Yes!"

". . . Grisman's, and while not actually treatable," a tiny man's voice said, "the technology is changing very rapidly."

"Dr. Grisman?"

At that moment, as if by design, or with the great simplicity of pure coincidence, the clouds broke across the Narrows, and the trapezoidal summit of Great Kills Peak emerged, for only a moment, into the sun—all green and gold. There was a flash near the top. The Pet Annex? A window? Then it was gone again.

". . . would make Grisman's treatable," the voice concluded. It was a recording.

"Repeat," I said.

Nothing.

"Hello?" I said; then, giving up, "Help?"

"Oncology Choices." A woman's voice. "How may I direct your call?"

"You already directed it. I was talking to a Dr. Grisman, but he hung up on me."

"Do you have a queue number?"

Luckily I had stored the one from the night before.

"Please hold while I connect you to the next available doctor."

"I don't want just any doctor, I want Dr. Grisman!"

But she was gone and the music was playing again. My leg was stiff but it didn't hurt anymore. I was having trouble staying awake. I knew it had to be the Cupper™. I stood up and hopped into the other room, and put the bra into the open dresser drawer, and closed it. But first I put my fist into the cup and watched the bluebirds darken, then fade when I withdrew it.

The drawer below it was filled with white panties, all alike also. The top drawer was socks, also all alike. I closed them all and hopped back into the kitchen. I felt my eyes closing as I watched the mists swirl around the broad shoulders of Great Kills, like a dirty shawl. Finally I got another voice, a guy: "Dr. Singh here."

"Is Dr. Grisman in?" I asked. "I think that's who I need to talk to."

"Grisman? Grisman is not a doctor."

"Vet. Whatever."

"Grisman's is a disease."

"A disease? What kind of disease?"

"I think you need to talk to Grief Counseling before we can have this conversation."

"I've already talked to Grief Counseling." I gave him, it, whatever, my GC access number.

"I'm going to connect you directly with Dr. Formentera in High Hospice. Please hold."

"Please don't . . ." But I was on hold again. Through the window I watched a train of trucks creep across the bridge. It seemed that they were creeping, but of course they were moving at ten or fifteen miles per hour. I imagined they were racing, trying to stay awake.

I toggled the phone display to headlines and scrolled through—

NEW LONG ISLAND EARTHQUAKE FEARS
SHOOTOUT IN MISDEMEANOR DEN
MAYOR CALLS FOR CLONE LAW CHANGE

Shootout!? Did that mean I was on the news? Unfortunately, I had only paid for headline (or Hi-Lites, as they called them) and couldn't access the text.

I was concentrating on the headline as if I might somehow coax more information out of it by staring, when I got a voice on the phone:

"Dr. Formentera here." Another guy. "Mr. Shapiro, I

assume by now you have heard the news. The bad news. The sad news."

"What!? You mean . . . Grisman's?"

"That's pretty much it. An intricate and very specialized form of brain cancer. Unique to man's best friend. There's something about a dog's brain, that faithful, loyal, loving biological wonder, that Grisman's finds irresistible. My theory is that it loves dogs as much as dogs love us. Of course, that's just a theory. Are you still there?"

"Yes."

"There's no treatment. Not yet. But that doesn't mean there never will be. I can imagine a world, and not that far off, where every disease of dog and man is treatable. Are you still there?"

"Yes." There was nothing to say. All my life I had expected the worst, and here, at last, it was. Cancer. I tried to visualize life without Homer. I came up with a blank.

"There's good news, though, Shapiro. Do you mind if I call you Shapiro? Are you still there?"

"Yes."

"Want to hear the good news?"

"Sure," I said. "I guess."

"Please hold."

There was a click, a brief scrap of music and then Formentera—or at least his voice—was back.

"The good news is that we have a special offer that will give your beloved pet a fighting chance. Can I take a moment of your time to tell you about it?"

Formentera sounded slightly different. More animated. More sympathetic. With that warm enthusiasm that only a recording can sustain.

"Whatever," I said.

"I'm sure you have read the stories about the modern medical miracle drug, HalfLife™. It was developed for an official government program, but like so many modern medical miracle drugs it has unexpected benefits for the general public. And for pets as well."

I should have answered here. They expected a response or they go into repeat.

"I'm sure you have read the stories about the modern medical miracle drug, HalfLife™. It was developed for an official government program, but like so many modern medical miracle drugs it has unexpected benefits for the general public. And for pets as well."

"I've heard of it, yes, I have heard of it."

"What would you say if I were to tell you that you, as a caring pet owner, were about to be one of the first to reap some of those unexpected medical benefits."

"Say?" Was it a question? I was glad he wasn't live. Most recordings don't care what you say as long as you say something.

"With HalfLife™, manufactured under license from the U.S. government, your beloved pet can be maintained until such a time as an appropriate and effective treatment is developed. And it might not take so long. Veterinary medicine is making tremendous strides these days. And now, are you ready for the best part?"

"Uh huh. Yes."

"If no cure is developed within a twenty-four-month period, your beloved companion will be peacefully put to sleep and disposed of free of charge. Yes, you heard me right—no charges, no hidden fees. Just a swift and caring termination to a long and satisfying relationship in which you will have the satisfaction of knowing that you did your best, that is, all that was humanly possible. Now, are you ready for the best part of all?"

"I guess," I said. I hoped the best part of all wasn't going to be as bad as the best part.

But it was.

"The best part of all is that it will only cost you 1250 to

maintain your beloved companion in comfort for an entire
year here at our modern Alpine Hospice overlooking all of
New York City."

That woke me up. "Twelve-fifty? But Homer's already
enrolled in MS-MD, as part of my plan."

"The plan is only until he dies. I thought you were interested in keeping him alive."

"She. Her. Yeah, sure."

"That's a policy extension. MS-MD's Pet Annex is for
treating sick pets, not for keeping pets alive when they have a
terminal illness. In fact, the HMO puts them under when
they start to suffer. Are you still there?"

"Yes."

"That's why HalfLife™ is only available as part of the
Alpine Hospice supplementary comprehensive protectional
extender. The 1250 is a modest copayment. We can charge
the copayment to your credit card. Are you still there?"

"Yes." Even though I was definitely having trouble staying
awake.

"To make the payment, which will effect the transfer to
the Alpine Hospice and begin the HalfLife™ regimen just
press or say okay."

"Okay," I said. "Okay, okay."

"Thank you," said the voice of Dr. Formentera. In the
background was a happy "woof woof," of dogs in a pen. I
listened, trying to distinguish Homer's voice. Then I realized
it probably wasn't real dogs but a recording. Promotional.
Homer wasn't much of a barker anyway. What Homer
mainly liked to do was lie in the sun and sleep, lie in the sun
and sleep, let the other dogs bark and lie in the sun and
sleep . . .

"Who are you calling?"

I had fallen asleep. I looked up. Henry was standing in the
doorway of the kitchen, with a paper sack in her arms.

Chapter 14

*T*he penalty phase of what was now universally called the Alexandrian Trial began with the reseating of the jury (plus the two alternates) whose appeal had been heard and relief, in the form of continued attendance, granted. The defense, in the person of Damaris, declined an opening statement and called the first of what was to be almost a hundred "expert witnesses" from around the world, using the relaxed rules of the penalty phase to finally make the Alexandrian case to the world. Writers, critics, museum operators, impresarios and entrepreneurs— all those who made a living on or around the great decomposing bodies of art, music, literature and film—pleaded the case that the Alexandrians themselves wouldn't. Citing figures correlating age and first publication, income and expectation, Hors Breen, art columnist for The New York Times, declared that "artistic overload" was destroying the drive and desire of young artists everywhere. Tateo Moldini recounted his campaign in Italy to rid the churches of Medieval and Renaissance art "so that a new Renaissance could flourish." Osiki Hade told of museums whose storerooms were larger than their galleries by a factor of ten. San Francisco talk-show host Gerry Bright spoke of the despair and apathy of the young, deluged with more books, recordings and films than they could possibly read, hear, or see. The parade of expert witnesses went on and on, prompting the Wall Street Journal to speculate that Damaris (as lead counsel) was trying to dramatize the very glut of information that her movement was on trial for attacking. Most attacked the overload in the name of art, but a few admitted frankly that they were there not to prune but to kill the tree of art. "It's time for humanity to occupy itself with new projects," said Sherry Netherland, the nouveau-punk art critic for The Glasgow Philistine, a newspaper dedicated openly to the idea that art was something that belonged (like Glasgow and England) to the past. Shockingly, but perhaps not surprisingly, no one on either side defended the permanence of art. Museums as well as individuals were being overwhelmed by a world which produced more, not less, every year, and in which even ephemera was preserved. The only people opposed to the actions of the Alexandrians were the relatives and loved ones of the individuals they had accidentally killed.

Damaris's summation, in which she called for an end to the "overload" of art and entertainment, was said by Variety to be her finest performance in twenty years, when she had played the part of a lawyer in Herod's Game. Her face was not only on the covers of the tabloids but in the opinion and news sections of respectable papers as well. Inspired by the trial (most thought) a new wave of bombings and "sloshings" (the destructions of paintings and books with nonexplosive but toxic liquids) broke out in European and American cities. It was one of these, the bombing of a video and game rental rack at a Colorado 7-Eleven, and the resulting accidental death of the clerk and her eleven-month-old son, that led to the first split among the Alexandrians.

Chapter 15

W ho are you calling?" Henry asked again.
I hung up. How long had I been asleep sitting up, listening to the un-dogs bark? Henry was standing in the kitchen doorway in her long skirt and bluebird sweater, holding a sack of groceries in her arms.

"I have a sick dog," I said. "What happened to my album?" I demanded. "Where am I?"

Instead of answering, she set the groceries on the table and started unpacking them. "Don't get up, you can't bend your leg. Do you want some tea?"

"I want to know what's going on."

She opened a package of those new bags that heat the water. She brewed us each a cup and sat down across the narrow table.

"You're at my place, obviously," Henry said. "In Bay Ridge. There was a shoot-out. Do you remember?"

"I worse than remember," I said. I toggled my phone to headlines and shoved it across the table to her, display up:

SHOOTOUT AT MISDEMEANOR DEN

She looked at it and shoved it back. "I saw the story," she said. "It's all lies."

I couldn't read it anyway. I only subscribe to headlines, not news. But there was no reason to tell her that. I pressed my attack: "You guys are in a lot of trouble. You lied to a Bureau officer. You stole an album. You kidnapped a Bureau officer. You took his hundred."

"What hundred?"

"The hundred I gave your friend Bob for the record-player. You can stop pretending he isn't a bootlegger. Or worse, an Alexandrian."

"I'm not pretending anything," she said. "And you should be thanking Bob for saving your life. You would have bled to death. He put that thing on your leg."

"The Cupper™," I said. "I know all about it. It's got those things in it that tell you. They also told me it could only be applied or taken off by a doctor."

"So?"

"So if he put it on me, that's another crime!" I was standing up, leaning on the table. Almost hollering.

Then I saw that the bluebirds were totally gone off her sweater. It was as gray as a cloud. Her eyes were filled with tears, about to spill over. In spite of myself, I felt sorry for her. Maybe it was the Cupper™.

I fell back into my chair, and lowered my voice. "Look," I said, "I never should have gotten involved in all this. I just wanted a record-player. I'll get my album back and go home. Where's my lectro?"

"Down on the street. Parked around the corner. I turned the floor mats over so the blood wouldn't show."

"Now all I need is my album, and I'm out of here."

"Bob saved it."

"So call him. Okay?"

"I never call him, he calls me. I don't even have his number."

"Do you have any idea how suspicious that sounds?" I asked. I was getting drowsy again.

"I'm sure he'll come by tonight," she said, making us some more tea. "You don't really need the album until the end of the month anyway."

"Huh?"

"Rendering. That's when Worth Street will find out it's not in the bag."

I was fully awake now. "How do you know all that?" I asked.

"I know because I'm an Alexandrian," she said finally. "Or almost. That's why I befriended you. The Alexandrians are always looking for contacts with Bureau officers. Then you walked into Charlie Rose High. I never thought it would lead to a shooting."

Almost an Alexandrian? The strange thing was, it didn't bother me. Maybe it was the Cupper™. Maybe it was the twilight gathering outside the window, like a curtain being lowered over the world.

"We just wanted a contact," she said. "In case something came up. Then you showed up with that record. Then they showed up, whoever they were. I figured it was a Bureau raid."

"That wasn't Enforcement," I said. "They don't even know I have the album. They don't raid misdemeanor clubs anyway. And they don't come busting in with Carillons."

"Well, they weren't Alexandrians," she said.

I was unconvinced but tired of arguing. She got up to 'wave us some supper, a Thai dish. It felt odd, being waited on. While we ate, and waited for Bob, Henry explained how she had gotten involved with the Alexandrians.

For love.

Something must have shown in my face. "Not for Bob!" she said. "For Panama."

"The canal or the country?"

"The artist," she said, sitting back down at the little chipped table across from me. "I never wanted to be a librarian. I wanted to be an artist. I even talked my parents into sending me to Paris, to art school."

"Paris, France?"

"Little Paris, in Florida. Panama was my instructor. He was very hard on me. At first I thought he was trying to discourage me. Then I saw that he was trying to keep from falling in love with me. As for me, I didn't even try."

"I can see that," I said. The bluebirds were back. I couldn't help smiling.

She looked down at her breasts and blushed.

"It was the old, old story," she said. "The coed and the professor. He thought he was different. I thought I was different. We even thought we could have a child." The blue-birds were fading. "Anyway, it all fell apart. We had been together less than three months when the school was raided. Panama barely got out the back door. I had no idea what was happening. I was as surprised then as you are now. I had been with an Alexandrian."

"So you became an Alexandrian yourself."

"I didn't care one way or another about the great art of the past, present or future. All I cared about was Panama. He sent Bob to tell me he had gone underground and to ask me to wait for him. That was almost nine years ago."

"And you're still waiting."

"I guess you might say that."

We were both still waiting—for Bob. We sat at the table and watched it get dark. It was like watching unseen hands decorate the city, hanging strings of beads, diamonds, precious stones, a dozen rings on every finger. One by one, then two by two, then ten by ten, hundreds, all at once, while the sky blushed pink, then rose.

It seemed, in the end, excessive.

Bob never showed.

"Something must have held him up," said Henry. "He usually calls. He'll call tomorrow."

She seemed about to cry, so I didn't say anything. We sat for half an hour more without talking, and then she went to bed in her bedroom and I went back to bed on the couch.

The next morning, the Cupper™ on my leg was still warm, though a little little less pink, and it bristled with short hog-like hairs.

I still didn't have to pee.

Henry was gone. She had washed and folded my sky blue, one-stripe pants and left them on a chair. They were almost as good as new, except for a tiny hole and a big rust colored stain just above the left knee.

I stood up and put them on—quite a trick when you can't bend your leg. But I was feeling better already.

I hopped to the window.

There was the lectro, around the corner, just where Henry had said. It was a windy October day; I could feel the wind with my fingertips on the glass. The leaves were blowing off the trees with a kind of suicidal eagerness. Great Kills Peak across the Narrows was clear, stripped of clouds. I saw an orange dot that might have been the Pet Annex and I thought of Homer, alone up there.

But she was all right—for now. The copayments were hard but not too hard. The main thing was to keep the insurance up to date.

That meant the main thing was my job.

That meant the main thing was to get the album back.

That meant the main thing was to find "Bob," who had never showed last night.

I was thinking of all these things when my phone rang. I hopped over to the couch. The number on the ID screen wasn't familiar, so I was hopeful. "Bob?"

"Mr. Shapiro? Hold for the doctor."

"Is this the Pet Annex?"

No answer. "Hold for the doctor" is often used for cold-call solicitations; it was even the title of a satirical Broadway musical revue a few years back. I was about to hang up, when a voice came on the line.

"Mr. Shapiro, this is Dr. Guttman. I'm afraid I have some disturbing news."

"Guttman? Are you Homer's vet?"

"More disturbing than that. This is Dr. Guttman in accounts. I'm afraid there's a problem."

"You got the copayment. I said okay. What's the problem?"

"The problem isn't the copayment but the policy. According to my records, you are a federal employee, on the George Washington TotalCare Delaware Family Plan?"

"Yes."

"According to your confidential internal TotalCare source file, the Delaware option has been deleted, which means no pets and no extenders," said Dr. Guttman. "We have therefore been unable to activate the supplementary comprehensive protectional extender as planned."

"Deleted?"

"Temporarily. While you're on Modified Duty."

"What's this Modified Duty stuff?" I said. "Hold for just a minute and let me call Worth Street."

I called Worth Street but there was, as usual, no answer. I called home. I figured there would be a message on my slate if there was a problem. But the line was busy. Did that mean Worth Street was trying to call me?

I toggled back to my previous call but now it was I who was on hold. I used the opportunity to hop into the bathroom and wash my face. I looked into the mirror for the first time in days and saw . . .

"Shapiro?" said a tiny voice.

I grabbed the phone. "Guttman? Put the HalfLife™ on my card for now," I said. "I'm still trying to get through to Federal Care."

"I'm afraid I can't do that," he said. "Under federal DNR regs, we are not allowed to keep any pet or client alive for more than twenty-four hours when it is suffering. Under our own industry's regulations, we are unable to process an extender or addendum when the primary account is on Modified Duty.

"Wait a minute—"

"Your beloved companion was moved this morning from the general population to the Farewell Verandah. His suffering will end at midnight. You will receive a picture in the mail, suitable for framing."

"You're going to kill my dog!?"

Click.

"Wait!" I said foolishly. But the line was already dead.

The stairs were long and dark, even in the daytime. I stumped down, holding my leg out. When I got to the bottom, I was shaking. My leg ached. I was afraid to look under my pants, but I had a feeling the Cupper™ was glowing with pleasure. It was hot to the touch even through the heavy sky blue cloth.

I limped across the street and around the corner to my car. I felt a moment of anxiety as I pressed my thumb into the lock—what if Worth Street had changed the locks somehow? It could probably be done by remote, electronically. But the door popped open, and I slid in and sped off, silently.

So far, so good. I headed for the bridge, going over things in my mind. The first part was simple: get Homer. I had until midnight. Beyond that, things got confusing. *Modified Duty.* Did that mean that Worth Street knew somehow that the Williams was out of the bag? Or did it simply mean they were waiting for me to check my slate? I had to get home. I had to find "Bob." I had to find the Williams and put it back into the bag, before rendering, which was at the end of the month, which was only . . .

"Pull over to the right, please."

I had been daydreaming—the Cupper™ again? I was at the tollbooth on the Staten Island end of the bridge. The EZPass lane light was red, and a bridge attendant was walking toward my lectro.

She tapped on my window with her slate. I was about to roll down the window when I saw the orange display on her slate:

Confidential: MODIFIED DUTY
Exercise Caution in Confiscation

"Pull over to the right, please," the attendant said through the glass, dimming the slate so I couldn't see it.

"Sure thing," I said, just to confuse her as I floored it. I pulled out into traffic, and left her standing there. I knew she wouldn't bother to chase me. The lectro was off the grid now, after jumping a red, and would only run for an hour at most. But that was enough to get me to the top of the mountain. I sped through the twisted streets, looking for a shortcut to Skyline Drive.

Confiscation? Of what? My slate? My bag? (Neither of which I had with me.) My lectro? Things were definitely going from bad to worse. But I had to keep my focus. First things first. Homer! I cried silently. Hang on, girl!

Twenty minutes later I entered the clouds. Two minutes after that I pulled into the Pet Annex lot. The building was a dim shape in the fog. I ran to the door and rang the buzzer. I couldn't see anyone in the lobby. I rang again. I banged on the glass.

"I'm a customer!" I said. Was customer the right word? I tried "client." I alternated them. I rang the buzzer with one hand and banged on the glass with the other. Finally a nurse came out of the shadows and approached the door. She kept her name tag covered, but I remembered.

"I have an appointment, Mrs. Quilvárres," I said. It helps to call people by name. But she knew it was a lie. She shook her head.

"No visits!" she shouted through the glass. She didn't even bother to take out her little kazoo.

"Please!" I shouted through the glass.

"Police!" she said.

"Huh?"

She took out her phone and started punching in numbers.

"Please!"

"Police!"

I coasted back down the hill to save juice. On the way, I tried calling home again but the line was still busy.

Then a man's voice answered. "Watchdog."

Watchdog? Had I been calling the wrong number? "Who is this?"

"None of your fucking business," he said and hung up.

Maple Street was named after the big trees that once graced almost every residential block in America, before the mad-tree disease struck them down. The house my father had "left" my mother, and my mother had left me, was in the middle of the block. As soon as I saw it, I knew something was wrong.

The driveway was filled with cars.

The shades were all drawn.

I slowed as I passed the house. It was filled with shadows, silhouettes, all men. I went around the block and drove by again, even more slowly. Two men were on the front porch this time, smoking cigarettes! They smiled at me as I passed; one of them waved; no, saluted.

I almost stopped to ask what was going on. Then on second thought, I floored it. The lectro still had enough juice to take me up the hill, over the end of Maple and back onto Victory Boulevard.

Then the amber light started flashing, and it was just as well. I pulled over. I could hardly breathe. My hands were shaking too much to drive. Things were going from bad to worse at a dizzying rate, and my brain was numb. Maybe it was still the Cupper™. I had to find a place where I could go and collect my thoughts, before I did something stupid, like knock on my own front door.

Luckily, there was just such a place only a few blocks away.

Where's your bag, Santa?" asked Lou after he had buzzed me in.

"Holiday," I muttered. I walked slowly over to the bar and eased up onto my favorite stool. I didn't want Lou to see me limping.

"What holiday?"

"All right, a personal day," I said. I realized I had made a mistake. I didn't want to talk to anybody until I had figured out what was going on, and more important, what to do. I didn't want to tell Lou—or Dante either, if he was there— about the Modified Duty. Or the lectro off the grid. Or the stolen album. Or the bullet hole in my leg. Or the cars in my drive. Or the silhouettes in my house.

At the same time, I had never felt so confused, so defeated, so blue. I had to talk to somebody, so I did the strangest thing. It still puzzles me, a little. I told Lou my dog had just died.

"Bummer," said Lou, cracking an egg into my glass. "Where is he, out in the car?"

"Her. She's up at the Pet Annex, on Great Kills Peak. And they won't release her."

"That's not right," said Lou.

"They're going to send me a picture."

"But you want to bury her, right?"

"Right," I said. "At home."

I hadn't even thought of it before, but it sounded right. I felt as outraged and as sad as if Homer had actually already died. It was like looking into the future, and then stepping in.

"Where there's a will there's a way," said a gloomy voice from the darkness.

"Where there's a what there's a what?" I asked.

"Dig," said Dante.

"The drug," said Lou.

"What are you guys talking about?" I asked.

"My brother-in-law Virgil is in what you might call the drug business," said Lou. "Also what you might call the junk business. He works both ends, selling dig to the miners working under Great Kills. They pay for it with the stuff they mine. You know dig? The drug?"

"I've heard of it," I said. "I don't see what that has to do with Homer."

"The mountain is honeycombed with mines," said Lou. "They dig up stuff for the flee markets out West. Barbies, shoes, housewares, car parts, plastics . . ."

I finished my bud. Were they changing the subject? "I still don't see what that has to do with Homer," I said. I was feeling offended.

"The tunnels go all the way to the top of the mountain," said Lou, helpfully, as he set another bud in front of me. "Underneath the Pet Annex. You know what I mean?"

"Don't bother him," said Dante scornfully. "They're about to cremate his dog but he doesn't want to know."

I shoved the bud aside. "You could set it up?"

"Sure," said Lou.

"My lectro's—in the shop."

"Not a problem," said Lou, punching a number into his cell phone. "They pick up and deliver."

It was two in the afternoon. Homer had until midnight to live. I drank the bud I had shoved away and ordered another. Maybe something good was going to happen after all.

Lou broke another egg into my glass.

"What's that for?"

"You're going to be out all night, walking through the tunnels. Crawling, even. Is something wrong with your leg?"

I was just about to tell him another lie when Dante said, from the darkness: "Hear that horn out front? Something tells me it's Destiny."

Chapter 16

*F*our of the eleven Alexandrians fired Damaris as
their attorney and announced their wish to
apologize to the victims. They became known as
the "Sorry Alexandrians." Judge Levy-Gomez-Ito
allowed neither their apology nor a change in plea,
although she did grant them a separate table. Through
a pro bono lawyer (retained, as it later turned out, by
The Loved Ones, Inc.) the Sorry Alexandrians sub-
mitted a separate petition to the president for a four-
part exemption to the mandatory death penalty.
Damaris not only refused to join in the apology, but
formally requested that each new crime be added to
the original indictment. Denied. After 114 days of
uninterrupted testimony, the prosecution was allowed
to make its case. It was simple and straightforward.
Nineteen people were dead, four of them under sixty-
five, which meant that their survivors were free to
pursue civil penalties. The Alexandrians had done it.
Period.

The final week was taken up by The Loved Ones,
Inc. In accordance with the Victims' Rights Amendment to the Constitution, each was given an hour to
speak. There were thirty-seven of them in all. Only
one (Lucy Blasdell, later rewarded with a contract on
Nickelodeon) recommended mercy for the defendants.
The rest spoke passionately of their losses, then sunk
once again into the obscurity that had never relaxed its
grip on them. Finally it was over.

At the end of the hearings, when Judge Ito-Gomez-
Levy opened the envelope from the president, reveal-
ing whether or not the death penalty exemption had

been granted, a silence fell over the courtroom that was broken only by her smile.

"Denied," said the judge, and she proceeded to sentence all eleven defendants to Death, Electrical.

Chapter 17

Destiny, if that was what it was, took the form of a bossy White man driving a long black lectro. "You alone? Sit in the middle, then. Keep your clothes on. Keep your hands off the upholstery. This is a Lincoln, not a grubby-hole."

Grubby-hole? I kept my mouth shut and my hand on my lap. He dropped me off under a streetlight in a grove of trash ailanthus on the north slope of Great Kills Peak. A worn path led through the trees to a low dirt cave. The October night was chill, but the rich-smelling fog coming out of the cave was warm.

There were lights. I stepped inside.

"You Shapiro? I'm Virgil," said a short, round man wearing a stained orange jumpsuit. "At least that's what Lou calls me. Was Elmo rude? I'll bet Elmo was rude."

I nodded.

"He thought you were a digger. He has an attitude. I hear you want to get up under the doghole. What's the matter with your leg?"

"An old injury," I said.

He tossed me a small sprayette, key-chain size. "Try this, on the roof of your mouth. It's for dead people but it's a pretty decent limb loosener all around. Go ahead."

The sprayette had a picture of a monk—two eyes peering out from under a cowl—and a logo that read LastRites™. It looked familiar; then I remembered the Walter Miller book I had picked up at the beginning of the week. I opened my mouth and sprayed behind my teeth. It was cold. It had no taste at all.

"That's enough," Virgil said. "It's addictive. Now give it back and let's get going."

We began our trip to the top of the mountain by going *down* a long, straight, sloping tunnel, about as steep as the aisle in an old movie theater. Boards had been laid down on the mud floor. My mouth was cold but my leg wasn't nearly as stiff. I could sort of hop along. The only problem was that my fingers wanted to interlock. I had to work to keep my hands apart.

Virgil carried a flashlight but it wasn't necessary. Our way was lighted by little gas flames, burning at the end of pipes that stuck out of the wall every few yards. The flares not only provided light, Virgil explained, but also burned off the seam methane and prevented explosions.

I heard a low, muttering sound up ahead. It sounded like an underground stream. It grew louder and louder until we came to our first pair of diggers about fifty yards into the mountain. Two men, both nude except for orange knee pads, scratched furiously at the side of the tunnel with short, blunt, spoonlike trowels. They talked excitedly as they worked. Their voices grew shrill when they saw us.

"Dog dish, ball point," they both said, pointing at the little red wagon between them. "Yo-yo, battery, knife and doll, spool, cartridge, beer can, plunger, wire wheel, candle holder, dental bridge, catsup bottle, stethoscope, plastic hat, computer mouse, TV antenna, horse shoe, paper weight, bus ticket, bread box . . ."

"Don't listen to them," Virgil said, pulling me away. "They never stop talking. Dig is like that."

"Paintbrush, broken comb," they murmured behind us. "Picture frame, roller, fish hook, pin, street sign, ring, hammer, D cell, golf ball, paddle, earring, Allen wrench, volume knob, arm rest, flower basket, eyeglass, button, cell phone, water bottle, modem."

Just before the tunnel turned, I stopped to look back. In the flickering light of the gas flames, the two diggers looked like denizens of Hell. Happy, chattering denizens of Hell.

"Where do they come from?" I asked.

"Elmo brings up two or three teams a night," said Virgil. "We provide the drug and the spoons. They decide where and when to dig. We just follow them and pick up the wagons."

The sound of their talking died away. The same murmuring rose and fell from other tunnels as we passed: "Toothpaste tube, crayon, remote, trivet, paper clip, guitar string, faucet, tube, model plane, broken tile, jewel box."

The mountain was as noisy inside as a hive.

Dig appealed, it appeared, mostly to men. Orange-suited miners, like Virgil, came and went like silent ghosts, collecting the filled wagons and dropping off empty ones. Others sifted through the filled wagons for dolls' heads, handbags, coins, bulbs, connectors, and other "valuables" that could be traded or sold. Still others carted the sorted debris outside, where it was dumped in long spoil banks on the side of the mountain.

I had been worried about the smell, but once you got used to it, it wasn't so bad. Sort of sweet.

The gas jets grew scarce. The murmuring of the diggers' constant talk grew louder, then softer, as the tunnels branched, first right, then left, but always (after the initial descent) tending upward. "Cord, cannister, shelf, shoe," they murmured as we passed. "Toy soldier, suntan bottle, trailer hitch, lighter, knob."

"Sometimes the good stuff runs in clumps," said Virgil. "Don't ask me why. Maybe it was dumped together, from a Dumpster outside a toy store, for example. Or it migrates, drifts underground. There are veins of treasure everywhere. There are dead spots, too, with nothing but diapers and picnic forks. It's all the same to them. They dig and we follow."

"And collect," I said, pointing at a wagon being rolled away. It was overflowing with dolls and dolls' heads, plastic shoes, Band-Aid boxes, tape cassettes.

"And collect," he agreed. "The stuff that sells changes from week to week, from year to year. From day to day. Depends on the flee markets."

I nodded, too out of breath to talk. The tunnels were ascending, getting steeper and smaller. My leg was getting stiff again. I could barely bend it.

We trudged, and trudged on. My hands started trying to clasp again—the spray—but it was worth it, for the pain in my leg was gone. The walls wept moisture, which oozed down into the planks and old plywood on which we walked. The floor rocked under our feet.

Twice we felt tremors, when a nearby tunnel collapsed. Each time, Virgil waited near a digging team until the danger was past. "In a *bump*—that's what we call it when a tunnel goes—the diggers are your only hope. You stay with them and follow them out."

"Handle, pot, frame, pepper shaker," they said. "Awning hook, tie pin, phono cartridge, fan blade, penny."

Only twice did I smell the loamy-acid smell of dig and never did I see the powder itself, which is always self-administered rectally. All I saw was its results—the diggers scratching away not at the earth but at the world that had been created by mankind.

"Do they ever dig in real dirt?" I asked Virgil.

"There is no real dirt," he said. "The entire mountain is made out of made stuff."

My leg was getting stiffer. I stopped and lifted it with my hands, and Virgil tossed me the sprayette with the hooded monk. "You don't want to use too much," he warned again.

Again I sprayed the roof of my mouth, and felt my leg relax. Again, I had to strain to keep my hands apart. Virgil was already moving up the tunnel, so I slipped the sprayette into the pocket of my one-stripe, sky blue pants. I was beginning to get the idea that it was valuable.

•   •   •

Virgil stopped for water twice. The orange-suited miners carried water in clear jugs, each with a cleaning root coiled at the bottom. It was for them; diggers never drank, never ate, never peed. All they did was dig and talk—to each other and to us, or at least to me, as we passed. "Wine glass, EZPass, helmet, piano key, nail," they said. "Collar, coffee lid, chopstick, string."

What amazed me was their happiness. Their faces held an intent look of expectation, like a kid opening a Christmas present, even though most of them looked as if they'd been digging for days.

Most of them had, Virgil told me. "Usually they dig until they drop, then when they wake up we give them cab fare. They always come back. They dig until they die."

"Talking," I said.

"The talking's just a side effect," Virgil said. "The digging is the thing. It's supposed to be the greatest high in the world. I don't suppose you've ever tried it?"

I shook my head.

"Don't. It's instant addiction. The digger thinks—believes!—that he is always just about to break through."

"Break through into what?"

"Who knows! It's about hope. That's the great happiness. You know the old saying, it's not the arrival but the journey. Digging is all journey. It's all end of journey but it never ends."

We were in a narrow passage lighted only by Virgil's flash, and I was wondering how much farther I could go before claustrophobia turned me back. A half-filled wagon almost blocked the tunnel; we squeezed by. My leg was getting stiff again. I couldn't get my breath. I wanted only to turn and run away.

"Here it is," said Virgil.

"Huh?"

I had to squat down before I could look up. Virgil's flash showed a flat iron door in the ceiling, shaped like a three-leaf clover.

"It's a drain," he said. "We found it by accident. I sealed it off. That's why there are no diggers up here. That's why the tunnel here is so small."

"The Pet Annex is up there?"

He nodded. "We call it the doghole. We hear barking sometimes."

"Will you wait for me?"

He shook his head.

"How will I get Homer out of here?"

"Homer?"

"My dog."

"Just go down," he said. "Be sure to replace the cover, then follow your nose, always going down. The tunnels all go down from here. They are all connected. I wouldn't say you couldn't get lost, but . . . you won't. And here, take this."

He handed me his flash. It was dim.

"Thanks," I said.

"Give it back before you leave." Then he slapped me twice on the shoulder and was gone.

I was alone. In the distance, below, I could hear murmuring, the endless talk of the diggers. And from above—something else. Dogs?

I wondered if Homer would be able to walk. Just in case, I emptied the wagon, which was only half-filled. One of the things that spilled out looked familiar. It was a murder weapon, a 9-mm auto. Rusted, corroded, pocked and pitted, but still recognizable by shape. We had studied them at Academy.

I slipped it into the pocket of my sky blue, one-stripe Bureau pants. It might come in useful as a hammer.

I could almost stand. I reached up. The metal manhole, or rather, doghole cover was cold. It was heavy.

I lifted it and slid it to one side. I stood up and climbed through. I was in a dark room. There was a sharp urine smell all around. I heard a growl.

"Homer?"

Chapter 18

*T*he Sorry Alexandrians were, ironically, the first to be put to death, being ushered into the Closure Chamber at 6 p.m. on December 4, 20—, four hours within the two-week maximum mandated by the Expeditious Execution Act of 20—, and several days before an appeal filed on their behalf (and against their will) was heard and—ironically again—granted by the president. The four died still apologizing over the speaker system that had been provided for that purpose, and their "corrected" bodies were exhibited for three days on the DOC's website, as required by law. The other or "original" Alexandrians' executions were delayed because of Damaris, who had one automatic and unwaivable appeal under the Celebrity Clemency Act of 20—, which provided for a four-judge review and a presidential hearing for anyone enshrined in the so-called "Walk of the Stars," regardless of their crime.

The prosecution responded by using their one allowed separation to remove her from the case, and her codefendants were expeditiously "chambered" late on the evening of December 11, 20—. The state paid a seven-day penalty. Like the first round, the broadcast had excellent ratings. Damaris was forced (the DOC said "allowed") to watch from the L.A. County Jail under the Visible Consequences Act of 20—.

While the president and his special cluster of appeals judges considered Damaris's automatic clemency petition, the bombings and acts of sabotage increased rather than diminished. The targets ranged far beyond the arts and entertainment, and included the *Spruce Goose* and even an unfortunate panda at the Washington zoo. Now it seemed that every group or individual with a grievance called themselves "Alexandrian." Attacks were made in the name of getting rid of European art, male art, White history, "mongrel" culture, and Jewish propaganda. A group calling themselves Alexandrian began a fast and sit-in at a recording studio in Hamburg, demanding a "recording sabbatical." The Internet itself was shut down for forty-three terrifying hours by a shadowy hacker conspiracy called alexandria.com. On January 12 (ten days late) Damaris was granted clemency by the president and resentenced by Judge Levy-Gomez-Ito to nineteen consecutive life terms in prison, prorated at twenty-four years each, to be served consecutively. The sentence of 456 years was the fourth-longest prison sentence ever given in California, and the longest ever given to a Celebrity. It was made possible only by the DOC's new drug, HalfLife™, which enabled prisoners in controlled conditions to live out their sentences.

Damaris's appeals had been exhausted and her property and credit forfeited (California #2545), and she was scheduled to be weldlocked into her cell at Journey's End, the vast new private prison in Vegas. A last-minute grant from a mysterious benefactor delayed the process, however, funding appeals of both her clemency and her sentence. In both appeals she asked for death. While they were pending, Damaris was transferred to a new, just-opened, maximum-security, minimum-amenity approach prison to await their outcome. That same morning, twenty artists and writers, musicians and filmmakers around the world (all of whom spoke English) received an electronic bank transfer, an airline ticket confirmation, and an enigmatic e-summons to "a major American city" for a top-secret two-week "cultural congress." They were to tell no one where they were going or why. Not one of the twenty individuals invited turned it down. A million is hard to resist.

Chapter 19

It wasn't Homer. It was a dog, though. Or dogs. It wasn't a growl as much as a snore, and it came from a lot of dogs.

The noise was all around me but I couldn't see a thing. I picked myself up off my knees, being careful not to step back into the hole I had just climbed through, and gave Virgil's flash a crank.

I was standing on a concrete floor, in a concrete room. Wire cages, stacked three high, covered the walls, except for a narrow door in the wall behind me.

There was a dog in every cage. They were all asleep. Most were snoring; some whimpered; others whined.

I started looking for Homer, cage by cage. My light beam hit a small terrier who opened his (her?) eyes and started yapping. The yaps were picked up by his next door neighbor, a big setter, who started barking. More dogs chimed in.

I was sure the noise would bring security. I hurried to find Homer, checking each cage with my light. All the dogs were awake now, and most were barking. All the cages held dogs except for one empty—which worried me—and three by the door that held the small designer "honey-bears" which had recently become popular.

Homer was in the corner, in a tiny cage at the bottom of a stack marked "Farewell Verandah," beside a glass-doored medicine cabinet. Her beady black eyes were closed.

"Homer?"

She looked almost too peaceful to disturb, in spite of the barking all around her. I was tempted for a moment to leave her there, and close the book on my life with her, on the legacy of my father (for she was a pup of the pup of his old bluetick hound, which he had left behind with mother and me). I put my fingers through the mesh and felt her nose. It was slick and warm. She was dying, I could tell.

Then she opened one eye and looked at me and whimpered. Her eye had changed; it was big and brown.

The cage was locked. I pulled the murder weapon out of my pocket and used it like a hammer to break the padlock. It took several blows; and all the time I was whispering, "Homer! Come on, girl! It's me, Shap!"

She stirred; she tried to get up, but couldn't. At first I didn't get it. Then I remembered the HalfLife™. Had they already started her on it?

I broke the glass on the medicine cabinet beside her cage. In the distance, an alarm went off.

Three bottles of pills said HalfLife™. There were also two small sprayettes with the picture of the cowled monk—Last-Rites™. I scooped them all up and jammed them into my pocket.

I could hear footsteps approaching, outside the door, echoing and scraping on bare concrete. Then shouts, coming closer. And in the distance, still, the alarm. All the dogs were barking now—all except Homer.

"Come on, girl!" I grabbed her by the collar and pulled her out of the cage. She hit the floor hard and groaned with pain, or perhaps fear. I dragged her toward the manhole in the center of the floor. My leg was stiff again.

I heard the door click. The knob rattled and turned. More shouts and scuffling of feet outside.

I pushed Homer through the manhole and jumped in after her, trying to land on my good leg and use it as a shock absorber. I missed and hit on my stiff leg; I staggered and fell over Homer in the dark. She groaned again.

Above me, a light came on. The dogs quit barking.

Reaching up, I pulled at the iron manhole cover. It slid

part way with a dreadful noise, then stuck. A crescent was still open, and I could see lights flashing through it; I could hear shouts.

"Hold it!" A beam of light came down through the hole.

I stuck the murder weapon up through the hole and tried to find the trigger with my finger.

BAM!

CLANG!

More shouts. The light went out. The dogs resumed barking. I slid the gun back into my pocket. I hadn't expected the thing to work!

I lifted Homer into the little red wagon. Her tail and head both hung over.

"This is security!" The voice echoed, as if it came over a bullhorn. "You are trespassing!"

"Not anymore," I whispered. Pulling the wagon behind me, I crawled down the tunnel, into the darkness. I didn't want to show a light. My leg wasn't stiff anymore but it felt hot, and wet, and sticky. I found that clapping my hands a few times as silently as possible weakened the clasp reflex.

As soon as we had turned a corner, I stopped.

Behind me I could hear a dreadful iron sliding sound. They were coming down the hole, after us? I drew the murder weapon again. I stuck my head around the corner, which was rough with splinters and wire.

The crescent of light was disappearing. They were closing the hole, not opening it. We were safe.

For now.

I gave Virgil's dimming flash a crank and pulled down my pants. My leg had started bleeding again. The Cupper™ was pink and glowing. I tried to peel it off—it was like part of my own skin.

The pain was terrible, but what could I do? I pulled my pants back up and stood, almost bumping my head on the filthy, oozing ceiling of the tunnel. Homer lay in the wagon like a big fish in a small boat, hanging over on all sides. In the light of Virgil's flash, her one open eye was brown and dull. Her nose was still warm.

"Come on, girl," I said, and we started down the mountain. On all sides, I heard the excited soft murmuring of the diggers. We passed a hollowed-out room where two diggers, both nude and scraped and bleeding, clawed at a section of wall. One seemed to be a woman, but it was hard to tell.

"Clothespin!" they said. "Spark plug, bottle cap, gum, dial, scissors, watch."

Soon we were in the zone of the gaslights, with their sharp smoky smell. I took one more small hit of the LastRites™. My hands wanted to come together, as if in prayer. At first I tried keeping my left hand in my pocket—then I tried pulling with both hands, fingers intertwined. That felt better.

My leg felt fine but I knew it was bleeding. I could feel the blood squishing in my shoe.

We passed several more groups of diggers, and miners pulling wagons just like mine. I spoke to no one, and no one noticed me until I found Virgil at the bottom, sorting trash into larger wagons and bins.

"You made it," he said. He seemed a little surprised.

"This is Homer," I said. "And this is for you."

I dug the two sprayettes I had swiped from the medicine cabinet out of my one-stripe pants, and tossed them to him. I kept the half-empty one for myself. I was later to wish I had kept all three. I was also later to wish I had given Virgil all three. As it was, I kept just enough to ruin my life and not enough to save it.

"Thanks," he said.

"Can I borrow the little red wagon?" I asked. "I'll return it."

Virgil nodded without answering. He was already tipping his head back and opening his throat for the spray.

•   •   •

It was cold outside the mountain—the first cold October night. I checked my phone—it was almost midnight. I had been inside Great Kills Peak for over seven hours!

My one-stripe, sky blue Bureau pants were wet with blood. The Cupper™ was still hot to the touch. Limping, I trundled Homer through the shabby, skinny, ailanthus woods and down the curb to the street. Pulling the wagon was much easier on the pavement. Though we were at the bottom of the mountain, it was still downhill all the way back to the D&D, where I had left my lectro. Hopefully, the batteries would be rested enough to get me home.

Wherever that was!

Homer lay in the wagon with one big brown eye open, but no one looking out; no one home. Whenever I looked back at her, pale as a ghost in the dim light of the streetlights, I hurried. Though what I was going to do with her, at the D&D or at Henry's, I had no idea. I was just glad to have her back.

The mountain loomed behind us like a gravestone.

The way back to the D&D led past the house. Actually, it was a block and a half out of the way, up Maple, which meant a sharp pull up a short hill. I was limping, and my shoe was squishy with blood, but I turned anyway; I wanted to see once more, with my own eyes, what was going on. Perhaps I hoped I had been dreaming.

I hadn't. Inside, as before, I saw shapes moving. The driveway was still filled with lectros with Bureau plates. Enforcement? I stopped the wagon under a tree, in the shadow of shadows. I remembered the murder weapon in my pocket—incriminating evidence, for sure—and slipped it into the wagon, underneath Homer. It woke her up; or maybe it was something about the house. Maybe she sensed she was close to home, as close—as it turned out—as she was ever to get again. She opened one eye and lifted her head as if to howl, and I took off running, with the wagon bouncing behind me. Homer never howled, but I never stopped running, all the way down the hill to the D&D.

The sign was flashing and the lights were on, but I didn't go in. I didn't want to see Lou or Dante either. I checked my lectro. The needle was in the yellow, but not yet on the red. I stuffed Homer into the front seat and put the wagon in the trunk.

The bridge is a free ride after midnight. My leg hurt again—all that walking. All that running. The Cupper™ was so hot it burned my hand—but not my leg. I had the feeling that my problems were spiraling out of control.

I approached Henry's building cautiously, looking for Enforcement cars. The coast seemed clear. Henry buzzed me up without asking who it was. I knew the elevator was pet-sensitive, so I covered the sensor with my hand so the door would shut—a trick I had learned from my mother. Perhaps the only one. My shoe had filled up with blood again and it was leaking out along the seams. I left little red crescent tracks.

Henry's apartment door was open. Ajar. The lights were off. I entered cautiously, fearing some sort of trap, and then I saw Henry sitting alone on the couch. "Henry, meet Homer," I said, closing the door behind me. She didn't answer. She didn't even look up. She was sitting doubled over, crying, and at first I thought she had been shot.

Chapter 20

*T*he names of the twenty who were given seats at the Alexandrian Round Table have never been published, although any knowledgeable guesser can account for several, and rumor and suggestion have implicated many more than could have been accommodated at any one time.

A few were world-famous (the number of Celebrities who can disappear for two weeks at a time, no questions asked, is surprisingly large). For others, honors and fame lay in the future. Most were and would remain obscure. What they all shared was an agreement and understanding that they would in no way attempt to capitalize on their membership in the group in any way, even by denying it.

The attendees arrived on a Thursday in a major northwestern city. Each arrived on a different flight and was met with a FedEx package containing a one-page agreement and a limo coupon for a hotel near the airport. The agreement explained the project and the conditions.

The project was described as an attempt to "systematically cleanse the canon without violence." The conditions were two: confidentiality and anonymity. There were two options, Accept and Decline.

Those who accepted were invited to a nine a.m. breakfast in the hotel restaurant the next morning.

There were no declines.

That evening was strange. The entire hotel staff consisted of six people who spoke no English, and indeed hardly spoke at all. It wasn't long before the attendees realized they were the only guests in the hotel. Some *were recognized, either through previous contacts or celebrity. But since no one was sure why anyone else was there, no contacts were made and the result was that everyone spent the evening in their rooms, watching television. It was an unusual and unusually pleasant experience for most.*

Chapter 21

"hat's wrong?" I asked.

I pulled the wagon with Homer in it into Henry's apartment, then closed and locked the door. I turned on the light. I had seen enough of the night.

Henry's eyes were closed and she was bent over. "What is it?" I asked again. "Did you come home from school early? Did you get fired?"

She nodded. "There was an assembly. A pep rally or a memorial or something. I seated my students and came home early. I didn't even punch out. I've never done that before."

"Done what?"

She groaned. "Not punch out." She wailed and clutched her stomach. There were no bluebirds on her sweater; it was gray all over.

"Stomach ache?"

She nodded, and I watched her eyes fill with tears. They splashed out as she swung her head from side to side. "Worse. I didn't tell you the truth!"

Was that all? "Is that all? If it hurt that much not to tell the truth, people would be doubled over all the time!"

I meant it as a joke but she didn't get it; at least, she didn't laugh. I went into the kitchen and got her two aspirins and a tall glass of water. "The truth about what?" I asked when I came back.

"About Panama. About Bob. About myself." She looked at the little pills and made a face. "These won't do any good."

But she swallowed them anyway.

She drank half the glass of water and handed it back to me. "Put a little whiskey in it," she said. "Under the sink."

Sure enough, I found a bottle of HeyGoodLookin' under the sink in the kitchen. When I stood up I noticed that my one-stripe pants were sticky and I was still leaving the little red crescent prints on the floor. But either my leg didn't hurt anymore, or I was getting used to the pain.

I poured whiskey in the water until it was light brown, and brought it back into the living room.

Henry looked better already. She was sitting up. I handed her the glass and she took a dainty, investigative sip. Then she took a long drink, looked at Homer, asleep in the wagon, and then at me. "Is that him?"

"Her," I said. "That's Homer. My dog."

"I thought she was at the hospital or something."

"She's—" I didn't want to say dying. "She's not getting any better. I brought her home. And what about you. Have you called a doctor?"

"I don't need a doctor," she said. She took another drink. "I know what it is. I need my pills. I need one a day. I get them from Bob. But I haven't seen him since the raid, the shoot-out. He hasn't even called."

I knew the feeling. "He has my album, too," I said. "What pills?"

"HalfLife™. For the baby."

"Baby?"

"Will you please stop repeating after me!?" Henry took another small sip of whiskey, then another long one. The birds were coming back: first the wings, then the little bodies. "Panama's baby. That's what I never told you. I'm pregnant. I found out right after he left."

"But you told me that was nine years ago!"

"Eight and a half, actually. Bob gets me the pills. HalfLife™, one a day. Keeps the baby from being born, you know what I mean?"

"Give me some of that whiskey." I took a long pull and

handed the empty glass back to her. "You've been pregnant for nine years?"

"Eight and a half, actually." She attempted a shrug, then groaned. "With Bob gone . . . when the pain started yesterday I got scared. But today . . ."

She doubled over with a new cramp and groaned again, a scary sound. The glass hit the floor and bounced. I picked it up and took it into the kitchen and filled it a third with water. I was just adding the whiskey when I heard a *ding* in the hallway.

Henry opened her eyes: The elevator.

There was a key turning in the door.

I turned off the light and stepped to one side of the door. I held the HeyGoodLookin' by the neck, like a club.

The door opened. "Henry?"

It was Bob.

I turned on the light.

"Where have you been?" Henry asked. "I've been looking all over for you."

"Wait'll you hear!" Bob was grinning. He closed the door behind him. Then he saw me with the bottle in my hand, raised to strike, and his smile faded. "He's still here? I thought he had to go to work."

"Am I glad to see you!" I said, lowering the bottle. "You have my album! Where is it?"

"It got—lost in the confusion," stammered Bob. "You know. Stolen in the raid." He didn't sound very convincing.

"Bullshit. Henry told me you had it. I saw you take it."

"I said he *saved* it!" Henry moaned.

"You told him I took it?" Bob glared at her. "It got lost in all the confusion. Somebody stole it."

"Bullshit!" I said, raising the bottle again.

Bob grabbed it out of my hand. "Let's have a drink first." He took a long swallow straight from the bottle and made a face. "What is this shit? Some kind of cowboy whiskey?"

"Never mind," I said. I handed Henry the glass and

reached for the bottle. "Where is my album? You stole it from me."

"Stole it?" said Bob, looking hurt. Or maybe it was guilty. "Not exactly. Oh, dear. I think I can explain. Just give me a minute." He took off his hat and sank down on the couch with a loud sigh. He was bald and his clothes were rumpled. He took another drink. Then he saw Homer. "What's with the dog in the wagon?"

"Don't change the subject," I said. "You stole my album."

"Did you bring my pills?" Henry asked, sipping at the whiskey. Though she was still complaining, I could tell she felt better. Her bluebirds were back.

"It wasn't your album," said Bob. "And you shouldn't act so high and mighty. You're the one who took it out of the bag." Before I could reply, he turned to Henry. "The pills are at my place, but I can't go there. I think I'm being followed. I know I'm being followed. Besides, I thought you had plenty of pills."

"I had to take a lot this week. I was getting those cramps again."

"You're not supposed to take more than one a day. They're not really all that good for you."

"I wanted to play the album once," I said, taking another sip of whiskey. "That's all. I have to get it back or I'll lose my job. Who'd you sell it to?"

"That I can't tell you," said Bob. "In fact there's nothing I can tell you, except that I didn't *sell* it to anybody. I did a public service."

"The Alexandrians," I said. I felt a cold dread. I was finished. I would never get it back—

"Ooooh!" wailed Henry, sitting down. She set the glass down on the floor and bent over double, like a jackknife.

Bob rushed to her side; he crouched down and put his hand on her shoulder.

"Ooooohhh!"

"I have some pills."

They both looked up at me: oddly, it was Bob's eyes that were filled with pain. I found it hard to hate him.

I pulled the bottle of HalfLife™ out of my pocket. "They're Homer's," I said. "I got them when I rescued her from the Pet Annex."

"It's pet strength," said Bob, grabbing the bottle out of my hand and handing it to Henry. "Take two."

"I'm way ahead of you," she said, shaking two pills into her palm.

"Leave some for Homer," I said. Then I thought, what's the point: if she was dying, why drag it out?

Henry gulped two down and chased them with the last of the whiskey and water. Then she coughed, wiped her little plumlike mouth, and handed me the glass. "Would you do the honors?"

I limped back into the kitchen, my left shoe still sticky, leaving crescent-shaped marks on the floor tiles. I was trying not to think of anything else, and almost succeeding. While I was pouring the HeyGoodLookin' into the glass, I heard a distinctive, familiar, ominous sound.

Ding.

The elevator.

Bob and Henry were frozen on the couch, both looking at the door, wide-eyed, waiting for the knock. But there was no knock.

BAM! The door burst open and two cops with shields rushed into the room. I dropped the glass but it didn't break. It even bounced once. I remember thinking it was probably made out of the same stuff as the shields.

A man in civilian clothes stepped out from behind the two cops. He looked familiar. He held a zipper in one hand and an electro-noose in the other. He spun the noose at me but it missed.

"Gggrrr!" Homer awakened, opening one beady black and one big brown eye. She leapt out of the wagon, sending it rolling backward. She lunged at the civilian's arm, taking it in her yellow jaw.

"Aaaargh!"

The civilian aimed the zipper at Homer and fired. Both cops fired.

ZAP! ZAP!

Homer went down!

The wagon had rolled into my knees. I saw the rusted, encrusted, pocked and pitted murder weapon in the bed of the wagon, where it had lain under Homer. I picked it up, closed my eyes, and fired.

BLAM! BLAM! BLAM!

Chapter 22

*B*reakfast was buffet style at a large table with twenty-two chairs. When twenty were filled, the secretive and eccentric billionaire philanthropist known to the world as "Mr. Bill" arrived. He wore a shirt and tie with jeans and sneakers. He appeared younger and better looking than in the rare pictures that had appeared since the breakup of his digital empire. He introduced himself formally, then asked, "Are there any questions?" There were. He answered them all, directly and candidly.

Yes, the cleansing process would have to be fair (even though the canon had never been); it was also important that it appear fair.

Yes, the Alexandrians would be represented. Precisely how was neither offered nor asked.

The process was to take exactly two weeks. It was to start immediately after lunch.

Another million would be paid to those who completed the project.

The results of the proceedings would belong entirely to Mr. Bill, who would use them in any way he saw fit. But the participants were to understand that they were designing a system for the world to use.

Mr. Bill would observe but not participate unless invited to by the group.

Then Mr. Bill said that he wanted to answer a question that had never been asked: how was the nondisclosure oath to be enforced?

He pressed a button on his palm computer, and two men in blue suits pushed a device into the room. It was about the size of a washing machine and it rolled on rubber tires. It was, Mr. Bill explained, a Tort Engine, plugged into every media and information network in the world, and programmed to monitor any and every mention of this gathering, its participants or its discussions, disagreements, goals, agendas, failures, and successes for the next fifty-five years. Any violation, no matter how small, would be met with a flurry of lawsuits certain to cripple and indeed bankrupt any magazine, television show, or publishing company, not to mention individual.

The Tort Engine was turned on briefly, so that the group could admire its rows of colored lights and, presumably, feel a thrill of fear. Then it was rolled away, and never seen again.

Chapter 23

I opened my eyes. The familiar-looking civilian lay face down on the floor, kicking slowly with one leg—*thump, thump, thump.* The two cops were backing out the door, their shields splattered with blood.

My hand was numb, and black with soot and powder. The gun had exploded!

I ran to Homer. Henry ran to Bob. They had both been hit—they lay head to head, their blood pooling into a single red mess on the faux-hardwood floor.

The two cops closed the door. They had left the civilian behind. He, too, had been hit, but unlike Bob he was still breathing. I could tell by the red bubbles in the pool of blood in the hollow of his back.

"Bob, wake up!" said Henry. "You can't be dead!"

"I didn't mean to shoot him," I said. "I didn't mean to shoot anybody. The gun must have exploded."

Homer's eyes were both open; one was beady and black and the other was big and brown. Both were brighter than I had ever seen them. Blood was oozing out of a hole just above her eyes. It was pumping slowly out of a larger hole in the back of her head. She looked at me pleadingly.

I stood and unbuttoned my sky blue pants.

"What in the world are you doing?" Henry asked.

"The Cupper™" I said. "If I can peel it off my thigh, I can use some of it on the bullet wound."

"I think he's already dead," she said. "He's not breathing."

"It's for Homer, not Bob," I said. "I can't just let her bleed to death."

"Why not? She's already dying of cancer. Wouldn't you be doing her a favor if you let her die?"

"Maybe," I said. But I didn't believe it. I pulled at the Cupper™ on my thigh. It peeled up just a little—and hurt a lot. I notched it with my fingernail and tore off a piece the size and shape of a Dr. Scholl's shoe insert. Tearing it didn't hurt at all. The Cupper™ was part of me, and yet it wasn't.

I slapped the patch onto Homer's head between her ears. It was long enough to cover both the entrance and exit wounds.

Homer closed her eyes. I pulled my pants back up.

"Bob, wake up! Wake up!" Henry was saying. But it was too late. He had a big blue mark on his forehead and the back blown out of his head. "He was my only friend! Now where am I going to get my pills?"

"Your only friend?" I said, surprised that I was a little hurt. "Didn't I just give you a pill? Besides, I'm in worse shape than you. He was going to take me to get my album back."

"Maybe he's not dead . . ." She shook him a little harder.

"He's dead and we've got to get out of here. Those cops will be back soon."

"You don't know cops. They're downstairs calling for backup. I'm more worried about the dead one."

"He's not dead." The pool of blood in the small of his back was still bubbling. "I'm not even sure he's a cop. He looks familiar."

I turned him over. He still looked familiar, but I couldn't quite place him. I turned out the light. In the darkness, I recognized him.

"Dante," I said. "What are you doing here?"

"You're a dead man," he whispered. He had a hole in his chest to match the hole in his back. Air wheezed and gurgled in and out. "Your girlfriend, too."

"Fuck you!" said Henry, leaning over him. "You're the one that's dying."

"You're all dead," whispered Dante. He was grinning, his teeth bright red with blood.

Henry pulled me aside. "Who is he, anyway? What does he mean we're dead? Are they Bureau cops?"

"Enforcement? I don't think so," I said. "I think we should get out of here, though."

"How?"

"My lectro's downstairs. The problem is, it's off the grid."

"And probably bugged . . ."

She was right, I realized.

". . . and what about your leg?"

"It feels better." I patted my thigh. The Cupper™ felt warm through my pants. Something was in my pocket; something small and hard. I pulled the little sprayer with the cowled monk on it out of my one-stripe pants.

"Wait! What's that?" Henry asked. But she already knew; she ripped it from my hand. "LastRites™—that's for dead people. Where'd you get it?"

I told her.

"Fantastic. It's for confessions and so forth," she said. "Last wills and testaments and such. You have to be a priest or a lawyer to buy it. Now I can talk to Bob. Help me out!"

"Talk to Bob?" I didn't like the sound of it. He lay in a big red stain on the floor. His eyes were wide open. He was dead.

But what other choice did we have? How else was I going to get my album back?

Henry sat on the floor beside Bob. She wrapped his head in a towel and held it in her lap. Then with both hands, she pried his mouth open.

"Go ahead," she said.

Reluctantly, I sprayed the roof of his mouth with Last-Rites™. I knew just what it felt like. But not for a dead person, of course.

Bob jerked and closed his eyes. "Oh no!" he said. His

hands came together on his chest, the fingers locked as if in prayer. I knew the feeling.

"Bob, it's me," Henry said.

"Who's me?"

"Henry."

"How come I can't see you? Oh no! Am I dead?"

"It's okay," I said, trying to help.

"Who are you? What do you mean, it's *okay*? Am I dead?"

"I guess. Yes," said Henry.

"You guess? I knew it! What's okay about that? What could be worse!?"

"Bob, you have to help me find Panama. I need him now that . . ."

"Now that what!? Now that I'm dead, right?!"

"Bob, It's not my fault. I'm sorry that you're dead."

"You're sorry!? Think how I feel!"

"This was not a good idea," I said to Henry.

"How come I can't see you?" Bob croaked. "Are my eyes closed? It's dark in here. Dark as hell!"

"You're on your way to Hell," I said cruelly. "Because you stole my Hank Williams album."

"It wasn't really yours," he said. "I'm sorry. I just wanted to be an Alexandrian."

"But you *are* an Alexandrian," said Henry.

"Not really. I'm sorry. But it's all over now," he said. His voice sounded dry.

"Not really!? What about Panama?" Henry demanded.

"Out West," said Bob. "Take the van. Henry?" He raised his head off Henry's lap. The towel fell away and I wanted to gag. The whole back of his head had been blown away. Parts of it were stuck to the towel.

"What?"

"It's over, Henry. I'm sorry."

"Sorry? Sorry about what?"

"I can't see anything. I'll tell you later."

"Later?! There's no later! You're dead!"

"Oh, no!" he groaned. "I knew it! And everybody else is alive, right? Everybody but me!"

"That's right," I said. I wanted to hurt him, even though he was already dead. "You're dead and you stole my album."

"Maybe it's not too late," he said. "Things got a little crazy but maybe you can get it back. From my brother."

"Panama?" Henry pleaded. "Please?"

"Take the van," Bob said. "Out West. Jersey. Fourteen on the Finder. But don't leave me here."

I heard something wailing in the distance. Sirens? "We've got to get out of here," I said. "Where's this van?"

"Around the corner," said Bob. "Fourth Avenue. Don't leave me here! Promise me! I can't believe I'm dead. I've been dreading this all my life."

"Okay, I promise," said Henry. She stood up suddenly, and Bob's head hit the floor with a wet thump. His eyes were wide open again. His hands were still locked together.

"He's gone," I said. "Gone again."

"Sssssh! What's that noise?" Henry asked.

I heard it too; it was the *beep-bop-beep* of a phone on autodial.

I looked in the hall. I looked in the kitchen. My leg ached again but I wasn't about to use the spray again, not after seeing what it was really for. Outside, it was getting light.

"Fourth Avenue," said a gurgly voice.

"Huh?" We both looked around.

"Dante!" I said. He was holding a cell phone in one hand and a charged, blinking zipper in the other.

"I thought you were dead," Henry said, kicking his phone across the room.

"You wish," Dante said. "Now you're dead. All of you."

She stepped over him and kicked the zipper out of his other hand. She did it expertly, as if she had practiced kicking guns and phones out of people's hands. "What is he, Enforcement? A bootlegger? A cop?" she asked me.

"An ex-cop, maybe. He must have been following me. Or maybe he was following Bob."

"Finished!" said Dante. "No matter where you go!"

"It's easy enough to find out," Henry said. "You can't lie on LastRites™."

"But he's not dead."

"I can fix that." Henry pulled a cushion from the couch and put it over Dante's face, then sat down on it.

"I don't think this is such a great idea," I said. Dante's arms and legs were flopping up and down, thumping noisily on the faux-hardwood floor.

"Why not?" Henry said. "You already killed him. I'm just an accessory." She bounced up and down on his face a couple of times, then picked up the pillow. Dante's eyes were closed and his mouth was wide open.

"Give me that stuff," Henry said, prying at his mouth.

"There's not much left," I said, grabbing her arm and dragging her to her feet. "Don't waste it."

I gave her the spray to shut her up. She weighed it in one hand, reconsidered, then stuck it up under her sweater. I was relieved. I didn't want to hear the truth, or anything else, from Dante.

I walked to the window. My leg was stiff and heavy; it was like hauling a stump around.

"I really think we should get out of here," I said.

Below, in the street, it was still dark, but to the west I could see the sun already glowing yellow-gold off the peak of Great Kills. They say memory only works one way, but there are times, like that morning, when you are already looking on the present from the future, when your life is already a memory. There's a glow to it, no matter how bad it gets.

"Unnh!"

I heard grunting behind me, and I turned around. Though I had seen Henry put the spray away, I half-expected to see

Dante sitting up. But no: it was Henry, trying to drag Bob's body out the door. She wouldn't leave without him ("I promised," she insisted) so I helped her drag him into the hall. Then while she waited for the elevator, I went back for Homer, fitting her carefully into the wagon.

Homer was looking better—or at least breathing more evenly. Her nose and the Cupper™ were both warm. And her eyes were closed, which was a relief: she has, or rather had, such pitiful, pleading eyes.

On the way out, I stopped to close Dante's eyes, but they were already closed. I held the whiskey glass in front of his face to see if it would fog up.

It didn't.

I could hear sirens in the distance as I closed the door behind me. *Ding* went the elevator. I cringed as the door opened; I half-expected it to be filled with armed cops. But it was empty. I cringed again when the door opened onto the lobby, and cringed again as we walked out the front door onto the street, carrying a corpse between us and pulling a dog behind us.

But Henry was right. There was nothing to worry about. The two cops that had broken down the door with Dante were sitting in a squad car across the street, apparently still waiting for backup. One was asleep and one was talking on his phone. He pretended not to notice us.

We found the van just where Bob had said it would be, around the corner, on Fourth Avenue. It was the same Gilette lectro with INDIAN BOB'S painted on the side. Indian Bob's *what*? I wondered.

It was locked, of course. For the first time, I was glad Bob was along. I held his head and shoulders while Henry guided his thumb into the lock depressions on the door. We had to do it again on the dash. The turbine whined up to speed. Lectros are only supposed to make a noise when they are engaging, but this one had a high-frequency shake.

Henry slid into the driver's seat and I laid Bob out in the

back, which was empty except for a few framed paintings in an upright stack, and a rolled-up rug.

I didn't see any record albums. But it was dark.

I lifted Homer, in her wagon, into the back, and wedged it between Bob and the paintings. "Let's get out of here," I said. Maybe it was my imagination, but I thought I could hear sirens in the distance. We were wanted criminals already—and wait till they talked to the cops waiting in the car, and saw the body and the blood upstairs!

"I'm trying to find the Finder," Henry said. She was studying the dash. "Where's the Finder on this thing?"

"Forget the Finder," I said. "Just head west."

Chapter 24

*A*fter lunch on April—, 20—, what was to be known (and unknown) as the Alexandrian Round Table assembled for their first meeting in the drab conference room of an ordinary airport hotel. There were no furnishings except for a round faux-oak table surrounded by rather uncomfortable blond wood chairs, and a thirty-three-inch television on a sideboard, which was dark except for a tiny light at its center, as if it had been turned off and had not yet quite shut down.

Though their names or occupations cannot be mentioned, due to the predatory and unsleeping eye of the Tort Machine, it can be said (and the fact that you are reading this proves that it can be said) that the members of the Round Table represented, directly or indirectly, every major artistic discipline (language arts, visual arts, music, film, etc.), every continent if not language (all spoke English, though not all spoke it as a first language), and every "race" if not every ethnic or religious group. Slightly more than half were men and slightly less women. More than a few were old, several young, and most middle-aged, that broad plain which we spend so many of our years crossing.

The question of the participation of the Alexandrians was raised once more. How could it not be? Not to have asked would have been to reveal by default what the reader has probably guessed: that several of the participants were either secret members or active sympathizers of the Alexandrians' various international clandestine formations. Mr. Bill's elaborate security was their only protection against the death penalty *which had been (at least potentially) extended to them all, courtesy of Damaris's "sacrifice."*

In answer, Mr. Bill clicked on the television with a whispered "frame on." It showed a woman in an orange jumpsuit, sitting on a metal bed in a tiny cell, staring at the camera. She greeted the Round Table in a soft, slightly hoarse voice, and a silence fell over the already silent room. Her voice was familiar not only from her films (which had enjoyed a brief revival) but from her trial. It was agreed that she would participate as a full member. If anyone objected they didn't say so, for Damaris could hear every voice at the table through the audio hookup to her cell. She couldn't see them, though. That didn't bother her. That was the way it had always been. The star on the screen never peers back into the darkened theatre.

The camera in her cell was not under her control. It sat in a high corner, out of reach, with a little red light that never blinked. Mr. Bill dimmed the hotel display at her request when she wanted to use the toilet.

More than half of the participants in the Alexandrian Round Table (as it came to be called) were European by ancestry, education, and inclination (including many who looked African or Asian), and this Western bias was the first objection raised—by the group's most "Western" members, interestingly. The first afternoon was spent discussing the problem, if indeed it was a problem. Damaris herself chaired this first session. It was decided that, whereas it was the West that had invented and promulgated worldwide the concept of Art as we know it; and whereas it was the West that had spawned the resistance, known as the Alexandrians; it was therefore the West that owed the world the cleansing process that would, it was hoped, put an end to both the information overload and the information it had spawned.

The Round Table seemed surprised, as the first day's discussion wound down, to find themselves reaching their first agreement. Looking back, it is not so astonishing, since they

*were being asked, in essence, to validate themselves and were
naturally inclined to do so. This first discussion accomplished
several ends: the "Euros" in the group were afterwards less
likely to assume either guilt or leadership inappropriately;
the Round Table saw that it could and was expected to agree
and to move forward. And Damaris was accepted as a full,
and indeed a leading, member.*

*The acceptance by the Round Table of its own constitu-
tion was the first procedural. The second procedural concerned Mr. Bill. Was he a member, an observer, a facilitator?
Or was he to be banned from the proceedings altogether?
This last option was raised by the philanthropist himself to
reaffirm his own sincerity and commitment to equality.*

*He was allowed to remain as a full voting member. And so
ended the first day.*

Chapter 25

"Wake up!"
I had been dozing, trying to ignore the pain in my leg. But when I woke up, there it was: a low throbbing. The sky was a dull pink, like bathroom tile.

The van was on the highway, in the slow lane. Trucks were whizzing past, rocking us in their wake. Something was *pop-pop-popp*ing against the windshield, a bug.

"We're being followed," Henry said. "The van is bugged."

"How do you know?" I asked stupidly. My leg hurt and I wanted a cup of coffee.

Henry pointed at the bug knocking against the windshield. It found metal at the seam between the windshield and the door, and stuck.

I looked closer. It was about an inch long, made of silvery magneto-plastic. Its wings, when it wasn't flying, disappeared, like the bluebirds on Henry's sweater (which were, this morning, only wingless shadows, like rockets in fog).

"Damn! Where are we?"

"Jersey. We just came out of the tunnel about a mile back."

"I thought bugs couldn't cross state lines," I said.

"Maybe it's federal. Or even international. Maybe they got an exemption, or an extension; or an agreement where the signal gets shunted to another bug. Who knows? Anyway, here it is."

"Was," I said. I reached across her and turned on the wipers, knocking the bug off.

"It'll be back," she said. "And whoever it is, now they know we know."

"Not necessarily. Maybe they just think it's raining."

I looked back. There were the towers of the city, insignificant against the towering dawn. The back of the van was filled with mysterious shapes, all gradually emerging from the darkness like toys on Christmas morning: paintings, corpses, dogs.

Everything but the album I had to get back. The problem made a dull ache, like my leg.

"Where are we heading?" I asked.

"Beats me," Henry said. She pointed to the back, where Bob's body was being gently bumped by Homer's wagon. "Bob said to hit fourteen, but there isn't any damned fourteen. The Finder said "TURN AROUND, TURN AROUND" until we got into the tunnel, then it shut up."

"TURN AROUND," the van said, as if prompted.

"And now there it is again!"

"Are you on fourteen?"

"I told you," she said, "there is no fourteen."

"We have to find fourteen, or else."

"Or else what?"

"We're screwed. You can't find Panama, I can't find my album, and we're stuck with a dead body."

"Well, first I have to pee." We were already in the slow lane. Slowing even further, Henry pulled into an enormous parking lot surrounding a tiny diner on three sides. "I need to find the little girls' room," she said.

"I'll wait here." I hadn't had to go to the bathroom since the Cupper™ had been put on my leg. That was, what? Four days? I wondered about Homer—did the Cupper™ on her head mean I wouldn't have to walk her anymore?

Henry went into the diner and I slid into the driver's seat. The Finder was a numeric pad on the right-hand side of the steering column. No map display.

It was a ten-key pad, with two bands, A and B. I hit B and

then four and the van said, "REROUTING, THANK YOU FOR YOUR PATIENCE." Then, "TURN RIGHT, ONE MILE. ONTO ONE AND NINE NORTH." Henry came back with two coffees and I pulled out into the traffic.

"TURN RIGHT, ONE MILE. ONTO ROUTE ONE AND NINE NORTH," the van repeated.

"Well, aren't you the wizard," Henry said as she tore a wedge out of the lid of my coffee, and then hers. I knew she was being sarcastic, but I did feel like a wizard after fixing both the bug and Finder problems.

Then we heard a *pop-pop-popp*ing against the side of the van: the bug was back. I decided to ignore it and just drive.

Now that it was daylight, or almost, I could see what was in the back of the van in my rearview mirror. Of course, everything in a mirror is reversed, so what looked like framed paintings, stacked upright on the left, were really a dog in a wagon and a corpse slowly but steadily rigor mortising into a cashew shape on the floor, on the right—and so forth. I didn't see any LPs or CDs at all. Homer was rolling forward when I braked, back when I stepped on the gas, the Cupper™ on her head glowing warm and pink in the dawn. Or was that reversed, too? Did she roll forward when I hit the gas? Was the sun setting? Was my dog dying after all?

"That dog always snore?" Henry asked.

"She didn't used to," I said. "Maybe it means she's getting better." Although I doubted it.

"EXIT ONE MILE ONTO ROUTE ONE-FOURTEEN NORTH," said the van. "WATCH FOR CONSTRUCTION. EXCEPT DELAYS."

"Oh no!" said Henry. "Off into the boonies!"

The road became a four lane, then a two. It wound past a few strip malls and a re-zoned subdivision, then into a low range of hills covered with diminutive hardwoods.

"The boonies," repeated Henry, finishing her coffee and throwing the cup out the window. I grimaced but she ignored me. "The boonies and then what?"

I shrugged. "That's up to you. All I want is to find Bob's brother and get my album back. I guess you have to keep going."

"So do you."

"What do you mean?"

"What are you going to do, go back to work as a pickup artist? Give the album back?"

"I have until the end of the month to find it. I'll take sick days until then."

"You're a dreamer," she said. "What about the cop you killed?"

"That was an accident," I said. "Maybe you're the dreamer, thinking you can find this Panama after he's been underground for nine years."

"Eight."

"TURN LEFT, ONE MILE. RIDGETOP ROAD," said the van.

Since neither of us wanted to talk, the Finder was a welcome interruption.

"TURN LEFT, JUST AHEAD. RIDGETOP ROAD."

I made the left turn, right after a billboard with an arrow, also pointing left:

RAMAPO CASINO
Wednesday Night is Senior Night!

"The boonies," Henry said again, shaking her head.

We were on a narrow blacktop road winding along the top of a low mountain. We passed a couple of burned-out houses set back in the trees. Each had a burned-out car in the drive. These were relics of the Asteroid Insurance Scandal of the late teens; or rather of the law that made cleanup illegal.

More signs appeared:

JACKSON WHITE
INDIAN CRAFTS

PAINTBALL
WATERSLIDE
NO-QUERY
GIFTE SHOPPE
HOMECOOKED FOODS

LOTTERY TICKETS

"You think all this has anything to do with the Indian Bob on the side of the van?" I asked.

"Duh."

"YOUR DESTINATION ONE MILE AHEAD." The Finder definitely seemed to be sending us to the casino. The signs got larger and closer together as we wound into the hills.

"TURN LEFT AT THE GIFT SHOP. TURN INTO THE LOT."

It was a gravel parking lot under the biggest sign of all. On one side there was a log cabin "trading post," and on the other a concrete teepee (or tipi?) casino, looking like the steeple of a buried church.

RAMAPO CASINO
JACKSON WHITE
INDIAN CRAFTS
NO-QUERY

Casinos never close. Inside, one video poker machine was beeping and ringing. Two women in sweat suits were sitting on a low bench, working the single machine like teamworkers on an assembly line. One fed in the coins and the other punched the buttons. They looked grim.

Henry went to find the "little girls' room." She seemed to be peeing for both of us.

There was a cashier window on one wall, barred like an ancient walk-in bank. Behind it, in a tiny room, a man in a cowboy hat dozed. He wore a tee shirt with a Geronimo profile and a slogan: ONE NOSY INDIAN. The hat had a beaded brim and a feather.

I tapped on the bars with a fingernail. If I had been wondering how I was going to find Bob's brother (and I had: we didn't even know his name), I quit wondering as soon as the dozing man woke up and lifted the brim of his hat.

He was Bob's twin.

"Do you have a brother?" I asked. "Named Bob?"

"Bob?" He turned slightly in the chair, and there it was! I saw the Hank Williams album behind him, propped up against the cash register.

"Excuse me, but . . ." My strategy was to get the album first, and then tell him about Bob. But Henry ruined that, returning from the "little girls' room" and shouldering me out of the way.

"I'm afraid we have some bad news!" she said breathlessly. "Bob is . . . that is, he was . . . that is, he has been killed. He was shot! Last night."

"Bob?" He took off his cowboy hat and punched the crown flat. Then he carefully straightened it and put it back on. "Which Bob?"

"Your brother," Henry said. "We brought him here because it was his last request. This place is on the Finder in his van. Fourteen."

"His van?!" The nosy Indian sat up, then stood up. He backed out of the change booth, locking the narrow door behind him. "Uh oh, I think I get it. Where is he?"

"In the parking lot."

"Excuse me, about that album . . ." I said, pointing at it through the bars. The Indian and Henry both ignored me and headed out the front door. I stared forlornly through the bars at the album, propped beside the cash register. Hank Williams looked more forlorn and lost than ever.

The two women were still feeding the slot machine. I could wait here, with them, in the half-darkness, or follow Henry and Bob's brother outside. On my way out I stopped to read the plaque on the wall just inside the door. It was plastic, but when I tapped it with my fingernail, it rang like brass.

> The Jackson Whites were a maroon community made up of escaped slaves and the Indians who took them in, plus a few sympathetic intermarried Whites. They lived in the tangled fastnesses of the tiny, rocky, rugged Ramapo Mountains of New Jersey through the Civil War and then the turn of the century, finally disappearing, like so many archaic communities, after World War II.
>
> After the Ethnicity Act of 20— provided them with a historian and an archeologist, a small community reappeared, engaged in the enterprise of researching their own histories.
>
> This casino is dedicated to the memory of those Jackson Whites who gave their lives for democracy in World Wars II and III.
>
> Ramapo New Jersey, el. 925 ft/282 m

I have always liked the idea of fastnesses, though the thin woods (rocky, to be sure) behind and around the parking lot didn't suggest or evoke it as a feeling. Probably the area had changed.

Henry and One Nosy Indian were already halfway across the lot, crunching across the gravel in the thin early morning sun. I caught up with them at the van, which we had left unlocked. Henry opened the sliding door and Homer opened one beady black eye and growled.

"That your dog? How much?"

"She's my dog," I said, from behind them. "And she's not for sale."

"I was just being polite," he said. "It's the Indian way. If I wanted a dog I wouldn't want one in a wagon with a pancake on his head. Where'd you get him?"

"Her," I said. I was beginning to get the gist of the One Nosy Indian tee shirt.

Homer was still growling, so I eased the wagon down, out

of the van, two wheels at a time, and pulled it around behind the van, into the shade. As soon as the Indian was out of sight, Homer stopped growling.

"Wait here," I said (rather foolishly: where was she going to go, in her wagon?) and went back to the side door of the van.

Bob's mouth was still closed. His lightless eyes were open wide. One Nosy Indian closed them with his fingertips.

"That's him," said One Nosy Indian. He took off his hat, smoothed it and put it back on. "I had a bad feeling when he left here last night. Who shot him, the cops?"

"No," said Henry.

"Yes," I said.

"You can say good-bye if you want to," said Henry, reaching up under her sweater and pulling out the Last-Rites™.

"I've heard of that stuff," said the Indian. "It's called the Right Stuff, right?"

"Right," said Henry.

"Does it really work?"

"You bet. Help me get his mouth open."

This was the part I hated. I joined Homer behind the van, in the shade. She was growling again.

"What is it this time?" I asked.

She lifted her nose toward the side of the van, meanwhile thumping the back of the wagon with her tail.

I had forgotten the bug. It was about the size and shape of a refrigerator magnet. I peeled it off the side of the van and pegged it into the woods.

"Good thinking," I said to Homer, patting her head. The Cupper™ was warm to the touch—almost hot. I went back around the van, to the open door.

I hadn't missed a thing. Henry and One Nosy Indian were still trying to get Bob's mouth open. Finally they managed with a spoon. Henry shook the can and gave him a shot.

"Oh no!" Bob, or rather the late Bob, jerked and groaned.

His eyes opened and then closed again. His hands came together, stiffly; I could hear his bones pop as his fingers found one another and locked together. His breath was getting bad. I could smell it all the way out on the gravel.

LastRites™ wrings the last scraps of air from the cells in the lung, and everyone is good for a few short sentences, depending on the condition of their lungs at the time of death.

Turned out Bob's were pretty good. "Am I dead? Oh no!"

"Bob, it's me," One Nosy Indian said.

"Who's me?"

"Robert. Bob. Something must have happened."

"You bet something happened! Something horrible! I'm dead and nobody cares."

"I care, Bob," the Nosy Indian broke in. "We care. We just don't show it. That's the Indian way. But I'll make sure you get a decent burial."

"Dead! What could be worse!"

"I can't think of anything," said One Nosy Indian. He took off his hat, smoothed it once again, and put it back on.

"Bob, you have to help me find Panama," said Henry.

"I'm sorry, Henry!" he croaked.

I'd had enough. "Good luck to all of you!" I said. "Just give me my album and I'll get out of here."

One Nosy Indian turned and looked at me, blinking in the bright sunshine. He adjusted his hat to shade his eyes. "Album? Oh, you mean the Hank Williams. Oh, so you're the guy."

"I definitely mean the Hank Williams," I said. "I definitely am the guy. And I definitely want my album back."

"Too late for that," One Nosy Indian said. "Are you sure you're not a cop?"

"He's not a cop," said Henry.

"I'll tell you about too late!" croaked Bob. "Too late is when you're dead and nobody cares!" His voice was just a whisper.

"Positive," I said. "And what do you mean, too late? I saw it there, in your office. That album wasn't his to sell to you. It's mine."

"He didn't sell it to me," said One Nosy Indian. "We're just doing him a favor. He wanted to do something for the Alexandrians. He was just being Bob."

"Just give it back, okay?"

"Too late."

"What do you mean?"

"Follow me," said One Nosy Indian. He started across the parking lot and I followed, but Henry called us back.

"Wait wait wait!" she said. "We can't just walk off and leave Bob."

"We can't?" the Indian asked. "How long does that stuff last?"

"It seems to be wearing off," said Henry.

"We'll be right back," I said. I had lost interest in Henry and her bluebirds. I had never been interested in Bob. I was only interested in getting my album and getting out of there; getting my job back; getting the cops out of my house; getting my dog . . . getting my dog what?

Homer lay backward in the wagon with her nose over the back and her tail over the front. She was dying of cancer and all I could do was stay with her until the end.

"We'll be right back," I said, patting her on the warm Cupper™ head.

I followed One Nosy Indian across the parking lot and into the casino. He didn't bother to unlock the cashier cage. Every other bar was a holo; he reached through and pulled out the album and handed it to me.

It was too light.

It was empty.

"They put the record in a different cover," he said. "Security, I guess. I liked the picture so I kept it."

"They who?"

"The Alexandrians. Who do you think?"

"Where can I find them?"

"Well, that's the million-dollar secret, isn't it? Vegas is the rumor, but who knows."

I followed him back outside, into the parking lot; into the sunshine. Henry and Homer were waiting in the shade behind the van. Bob was dead again; he was curled up like a cashew, on his side. His eyes were wide open and he was starting to smell, just a little.

"That was Bob for you," said One Nosy Indian. "Bob wanted to give them the album for nothing. All we did was put it into the pipeline. It goes from here to another brother, Bob, out West. It eventually gets to the Alexandrians. That's the idea, anyway."

"Two brothers both named Bob?"

"It's an Indian thing. But that's neither here nor there," he said. "Tell you what I'm going to do. I'm going to make you an offer you can't refuse. You can have the van, and all the stuff in it, as long as you take Bob's body to his other brother to be buried. We can't do anything for him here."

"Other brother Bob?" asked Henry. "Where?"

"You'll find him somewhere on the way to Vegas. Nebraska, or maybe it's Iowa."

"You don't even know where?" Henry asked. She was beginning to get, or at least sound, pissed. But I was intrigued. Nebraska—Iowa—Vegas! They were all out West.

"It's on the Finder, eight or nine. Try nine first."

"Maybe you should throw in expenses."

I was shocked at Henry's boldness and greed. At first it seemed that One Nosy Indian was, too. He turned on his heel and walked across the parking lot, into the casino—then came right out with a stack of red, white, and blue chips.

"Chips!?" Henry was still playing hard to get.

"Better than gold," he said, reaching through the window and placing them on the dashboard of the van. Later, I was to wish he had told us what each color was worth.

"Adios, Kemosabe," he called after us as we drove off.

Chapter 26

Which of the arts were to be cleansed? Were any to be spared? Were the disciplines to be linked or separated? Were certain classics to be exempted, or should everything ever produced be put under the knife? Who would choose what stayed and what went? Should the prejudices of the past (racial, ethnic, gender, religious, cultural) be preserved, or discarded; or modified, corrected? What about the unrecognized (and recognized) prejudices of the present? It was suggested that such large questions be dealt with in the concrete rather than the abstract; otherwise the group would spend all its time on questions, and little on answers.

And so the Round Table began where the Alexandrians themselves had begun, with oil painting, a particularly European discipline. Once the queen of the Arts, it still held a great prestige even though little new work of note was produced. It was decided that paintings to be deleted were to be chosen by lot, and destroyed along with all their copies, digital and print, even to the tiniest illustration in an art history book or database. It was observed that to delete paintings one by one would be unfair to the less prolific, and ridiculous in the case of a painter who, like, say, Monet, often painted numerous versions of the same scene. Answer: it was the artist who was to be deleted—all his (or her) works at once. It was at this point that a shudder went around the Round Table as, one by one, the group realized the enormity—the finality—of what they were proposing. It was like (one said) watching a new planet swim onto view (or out, quipped another).

What of Rembrandt? What of Michelangelo? What of Michelangelo indeed, was the answer. Wasn't Michelangelo precisely the problem? Wasn't it the aim of the Alexandrians and the task of this group to clear the space for the next Michelangelo, the next Rembrandt, the next Monet? As the debate raged, the Round Table relived in every detail, in sequence, the shock, the fascination, the acceptance, the approval, and the liberatory exuberance the world had felt with the appearance of the Alexandrians. Burn the barn! The reluctant were won all the way to eagerness; the ambivalent became passionate; the cautious became confident.

Burn the Barn! Kick out the Jams!

One more question: once all the digital and print repros had been hunted down and scoured and cleansed, should the presumably irreplaceable originals be destroyed—or just pulled out of circulation?

Destroyed! The last thing the world needed was more half measures.

Chapter 27

"TURN LEFT ONTO RIDGETOP ROAD," said the van as I pulled out of the lot, left, onto Ridgetop Road, heading west. The Finder was set on nine. It was nothing more than a guess.

Henry sat staring through the windshield, west, with a grim rather than hopeful look on her face. The bluebirds on her sweater looked like rocket bombs, wingless and eyeless.

"Here we go!" I said, trying to sound cheerful as the turbine whined up to off-grid max, about a hundred kph.

"Like where?" she said.

"West!" I replied. "We're going to find my LP. We're going to find Bob's brother. Other brother. We're going to find what's his name, Panama."

"How's that?" she asked gloomily.

"He's an Alexandrian, isn't he? When we find my album we find him."

"In a bugged van."

"I took care of that," I said. And indeed I thought, at the time, that I had.

We drove in silence for twenty minutes, down a twisting mountain road, until the van spoke up again: "PREPARE TO TAKE I-80 WEST IN ONE MILE."

That was a relief. The van could only go for about a hundred miles off the grid, and we had logged almost eighty between the tunnel, the casino, and the interchange we were now approaching.

"ENTRANCE RAMP TO I-80 WEST, ONE QUARTER MILE."

I liked West. "What if the Alexandrians are in Vegas?" I mused aloud.

"Not very likely," Henry grumbled.

Still . . . Vegas, the only city in America you had to have a ticket to enter. Except, of course, it's not exactly *in* America. "Do you have any idea how far it is to Vegas?" I hadn't been west of the Hudson since I was a kid, and now we were heading all the way across the Mississippi.

"I'm a teacher," Henry said. "It's 3,589. That's from Brooklyn. Subtract about a hundred."

"Miles or kilometers?"

"Kilometers. It's twice as far in miles," she said. "Either twice or half. Anyway, it's a long way." She closed her eyes.

"Are you okay?"

"I think I need another pill," she said.

I gave her one and she swallowed it, washing it down with her own spit as I drove onto the ramp and onto the grid. She closed her eyes and moaned. Homer kept one eye open and snored. The Cupper™ seemed to have given her the ability to sleep with one eye open, but always the same one, the beady black one. Her little red wagon rocked gently back and forth as the van merged smoothly with a stream of truck-trains heading west. Like Lincoln, we crossed the Delaware. The low ridges parted before the highway like waves. The first Pennsylvania toll was easy—we slid right through. It was the end of the month, though, and I was worried. The EzGo covered the highway and the current, but when it was gone we would have to come up with cash.

All we had were chips, the little stack of reds, whites, and blues. I set them on the narrow dash and counted them as I "drove" (all the grid requires is a butt on the seat). Twelve all together. I figured they were tens, fifties, and hundreds, and I tried to guess which color was which. But I couldn't make them come out right.

It took us all day to cross Pennsylvania, a state of long low mountains that looked flat-topped unless you saw them edge on, which was almost never. I never saw more than one mountain at a time, and they all looked the same: long straight ridges as smooth on the top as art made by kids, or widows. Except for the van's periodic "CARRY ON," no one spoke. One Nosy Indian and Bob had talked enough for us both. The silence was welcome.

We made several stops for "little girls' rooms" and one for a sandwich, which I bought with the last of our money. Now we were down to nothing but chips, which meant we had to find a flee market, which meant we had to be near a state line.

The empty album cover, wedged under the dash, stared me in the face. I had to fill it by the end of the month to get my job back. But would that get the police out of my house; explain my presence at the misdemeanor club (if it had been noticed) or at Henry's apartment; or explain the body still (for all I knew) on her floor? All I could think of was getting the LP back into the sleeve. It's hard to remember exactly what we were thinking at any one time. The narratives that stitch our lives together ("I wanted to get married," "I was trying to get a better job," "I was trying to get away from mother") are all creations of memory. And some say consciousness itself is memory—that we are always living a few seconds in the past, like plants eternally slipping off a ledge into the holding, forgiving, thin air.

"CARRY ON," said the Finder, every twenty minutes or so. I didn't mind "driving" and Henry seemed to need her sleep. Pennsylvania is a long state. It was an uneventful day until late afternoon. We were just coming down the long western slope of Blue Mountain, the last (as it turned out) of Pennsylvania's long parallel ranges, when I heard a sound like gravel rattling against the side of the van:

Pop-pop-pop!

I knew what it was right away. The bug.

Henry's eyes were closed and she either didn't hear, or was pretending not to hear. So I said nothing, not wanting to wake her, or alarm her. "CARRY ON," said the Finder. After a while Henry woke up on her own: she opened one eye and

THE PICKUP ARTIST   133

then the other, moaned, groaned, got up from the seat and went to the back. She seemed to be waddling a little or was it the motion of the van? She rolled up in the rug next to Bob, and soon I could hear her snores mixing with Homer's.

Since they are prohibited by the Sumptuary Laws from staying more than one day in a state, flee markets tend to cluster along the state lines. I knew we were approaching Ohio when I saw the blue and orange "no-query" flags over a field separated by a dry ditch from a broad expanse of corn stubble. I saw the flags before I saw the exit, which I almost missed.

I pulled off the grid and then off the ramp and then off the road. The van bounced into an unpaved parking lot. I saw lots of tables but few customers. "Where are we?" Henry asked, sitting up. I told her.

I parked alongside the dry ditch, in a long line of other vans. Henry unrolled herself and set off to look for a "little girl's room" while I opened the side door of the van to unload Homer.

She opened her beady black eye, and growled.

I turned and saw a small man in a blue and orange uniform, holding a clipboard and a paper bag. "Who's that?" he asked.

He was staring at Bob, who was curled up like a cashew and starting (I realized) to stink.

"That's my brother," I said. "I'm taking him home to be buried."

"You can't bury anybody here," he said. "State line."

"I'm just stopping by," I said. "Saw the flags."

"There's a fee for selling here," he said.

"We're just here to buy."

"Fee for buying, too. And parking."

"I don't have any cash," I said.

He saw the chips on the dash. "Are those UIC?" He meant United Indian Casinos.

I nodded and he reached in the window and took a blue

one off the top. "There's a fee for building a fire, too," he said, taking another. Henry had just returned with an armload of twigs.

"I'm not building a fire," she said. "I'm building a dog house. Is there a fee for that?"

"No, there's not."

"Good, then you can put that back." She let the twigs fall with a feathery crash and stared at the man until he handed the second blue chip to me, and left.

"What was that all about?" she asked me.

"Bob," I said. We straightened him out as best we could and rolled him up in the rug. Homer watched; I could tell she wasn't asleep because she wasn't snoring. The Cupper™ on top of her head was warm to the touch. I liked patting it better than I liked patting her. That made me feel guilty, just a little. "How about you and me taking a walk?" I said.

We left Henry behind to build a fire (we thought), and I pulled Homer behind me through the flee market, looking for a no-query who would trade chips for cash. We needed food and we needed pills for Henry. There were few customers. The vendors stood behind their tables eyeing one another with a mixture of suspicion and longing. The tables were set into groups that supposedly held different kinds of merchandise, though they all seemed the same. Knives and tools segued into bottles, household goods, glass and dishes; furniture led to toys and toys to weaponry, both real and imaginary.

The only no-query was in a booth near Patches, Medals & Badges. "This is UIC," she said, wiping off her tiny blue and orange badge as she studied the blue chip, front and back. "No good east of the Mississippi or west of the Delaware."

"I thought you were a no-query," I said.

"I'll have to discount it by half. But I'll give you fifty-five because I like dogs."

I nodded; it was getting dark and I was getting hungry. She handed me fifty-five in treasury notes. On the one hand it hurt to realize how badly we had been ripped off by the official with the clipboard; on the other hand it felt good to realize how much the chips were worth. At least the blue ones.

"I'll give you another fifty for that baby," the no-query said, pointing behind me.

"Homer's not for sale."

"I don't mean the dog, I mean the wagon. The Radio Flyer™."

"I don't think so," I said, and left, even though she called after me—"A hundred!" I found pharmaceuticals, on a table near Badges & Medals, but there was no HalfLife™, and indeed no LastRites™. Dig was plentiful and cheap, a change from New York, where it had been (according to Dante) dear.

Dante. I wondered if he had been found. I didn't like to think about Dante. It reminded me how far I was from home, my job and my life. What was I doing here, in this field of corn stubble and wobbly tables?

I was brought back to reality by the sight of another customer: a cute, or fairly cute girl, or woman, with short hair and full breasts, and . . . then she turned to face me and I saw it was Henry.

"What are you doing here?"

"Looking for pills," she said. "I haven't found any but I found this."

She handed me a bottle of whiskey and a warm package about the size of a small dog. When Homer saw it, she growled.

"Bush meat," she said. "For dinner."

I put the bush meat and the whiskey in the wagon next to Homer, and headed back to the van, while Henry set off to find the "little girls' room." Back at the van, I remembered the bug. They are said to have a learning algorithm for concealment, and I found it not on the side of the van where it had hit, but underneath, where the sheet metal tucks under the frame.

This time, I looked at it with more care. It was about an inch long, with a two-inch span of silicon wings. The only sign of life was the flashing red eye. Destroying the bug was out of the question, unless I wanted a civil murder charge added to the capital murder that (probably) already awaited me due to Dante's death. But I had to get rid of it somehow.

I was still trying to think of a way when I saw Henry returning, doubled over with cramps, and I stuck the bug into my pants pocket. Flashing red eye and all.

Henry squatted down and poked the fire with a stick, moaning.

"Are you okay?" I asked.

"No."

"What is it?"

"You know what it is."

The bottle with Homer's HalfLife™ was in my other pocket, the one without the bug. I gave her two.

"Let me keep the bottle." She reached for it.

I pulled it back. "They're Homer's."

"He doesn't need them," she said.

"She." But she was right. Homer seemed fine without them, and getting better. But I kept the bottle. There were only four left.

The meat was still warm, and hardly needed cooking. Homer didn't object to it unwrapped, but she still didn't seem to want to eat. The whiskey was HeyGoodLookin', the same brand I had (almost) brained Bob with. After we ate we sat up and talked.

Everyone's life is a tapestry of disappointments. Mine had to do more with my mother than with my father, who hadn't stayed around long enough to disappoint me. And my job, or former job. Henry's had to do with the elusive Panama, and lately, with Bob.

"I know Panama will want to find me, now that Bob is dead," she said. I listened in silence. It seemed ungenerous to point out that it was she who was finding Panama, not the other way around.

The flee market at night is a strange and spooky place. We heard muddled shouts, short screams, dogs howling. Homer twitched in her wagon and groaned. Henry and I sat shoulder to shoulder, the strangeness of the night and the sounds knitting us closer together than the long day's drive had done. I put my arm around her plump shoulders until she fell asleep. Then I wrapped her in the rug next to Bob on the hard metal floor of the van. I slept outside by the fire, sitting up. I didn't want anyone getting the idea that our van was there for anyone to break into or steal—even though I saw no one, only heard voices and footsteps and, occasionally, blows.

I must have slept, for when I awakened the moon was down. It was pitch dark. The air was cold with a touch of winter, that little death of the world. The stars were like pinpricks, letting us see the light from but not the shape of the world beyond this one. It was a mystery. I had an erection, my first in years. Something was fluttering in my pants . . .

I jumped up, wide awake—I had forgotten the bug I had peeled off the bottom of the van!

It was time to get rid of it; night seemed the best time for the sort of skullduggery I had in mind. A plastic bag blew by, serendipitously completing my plan. I snagged it and wrapped the bug in it. I crossed the ditch and dug a hole in the mud bank with a stick, and buried the bug. I tamped it down but not too tight. Who knew what would set off the "murder" alarms back in the office of whichever agency had sent it?

I unrolled Henry just enough to borrow a little of her rug, and went back to sleep. When I woke up, she was sitting by the fire, sipping from a Styrofoam cup. She made a face and held out her hand, and I gave her two HalfLife™ pills without making her ask.

That left two.

She swallowed them, washed them down, and passed me the cup.

"Coffee?"

"I took a chip off the dash," she said. "Somebody was selling it."

"White?"

She nodded. I moaned.

"That coffee cost sixty-five!" I said. "A hundred, really."

She had a different perspective. "Forget the ones we've spent. We still have a bunch, and they must be worth a lot. Once we cross the Mississippi we will be rich."

She had a point. I didn't feel like arguing anyway.

The air was cold and filled with unfamiliar sounds—cars and trucks, many of them probably gas-o-line, starting up; good-byes and farewells; the *bam-snick-snack* of folding tables. The flee market was leaving.

Henry and I shared the rest of the coffee and watched them pull out, across the fields in a long single line. By the time the sun cleared the trees to the east, the flee market was gone, except for a few old ladies with plastic bags going through the trash.

It was Monday morning. I called in sick, and punched in a repeat that would call in sick every morning until the end of the month.

Homer seemed better. The Cupper™ on her head was alarmingly warm, but her nose was cold. Both her eyes were closed and her breathing was regular. I knew it was just an illusion but I didn't care. At least she wasn't suffering.

"Give me a hand," Henry said from inside the van. She meant it literally. She had unwrapped Bob and was struggling to straighten out his arm to reach the ignition pad. I helped her; his arms were as stiff as wire, but as bendable.

Together we pressed his fingertips into the depression on the dash. The turbo whined up, and we were off.

"TAKE THE INTERSTATE WEST," said the Finder. Henry drove. We bounced across corn stubble, following the broad track the flee market's vehicles had made, looking for an entrance ramp. The almost-empty highway, washed by the rain and bright in the sun, made a line like an arrow, pointing west.

"WEST ON INTERSTATE 80."

Nine on the Finder.

Chapter 28

O il painting turned out to be the web that held all the visual arts, since few artists work in only one medium. An artist's watercolors and sketches followed his oils (and frescoes and murals) into oblivion. Unsigned went with signed (anticipating evasions and abuses). Sculpture as a discipline was decidedly uncrowded, and yet so permanent that it, too, needed to be cleansed. Photography was exempted, since there was no reliable way to separate out those photographs that aspired to the status of art. This was to lead to elaborate and often entertaining abuses, such as the "snapsters" who made oil paintings, photographed them, and then destroyed the originals in the hope that their works would not be deleted. The exemption of commercial art (without signature or attribution) was also to lead to abuse: there was the "Warhol of 55th Street," whose menu drawings at the Russian Tea Room were too clever by half, being remembered long after the man who created them.

And what of direct noncompliance? What if the deleted artist simply refused to stop working? He or she could be killed; this was suggested not as a cruelty but as a kindness. But a far simpler and even kinder method suggested itself: only dead artists were to be deleted. Thus immortality would be, for the dying artist, the same crapshoot it had always been. This first distinction between the living and the dead was to prove the crack through which the concept of the Immortals entered the equation.

But not yet. First came literature.

Chapter 29

"CARRY ON," said the Finder.

It would only change if there was a change.

Interstate 80 followed the broad, flat top of Ohio across the endless marshy fields of nearbeans, supercorns, and neo-sorghums. Waving fields of faux grains. While Henry "drove," I straightened the back of the van. Bob, rolled up in the rug, was getting stiffer and stiffer, though I had to admit he was starting to smell less and less rather than more and more. Or were we just getting used to it? We had left his right hand extended over his head, so that we could use him like a key to start the van. It looked like he was waving good-bye.

Good-bye!

My leg felt better than ever. The Cupper™ was almost gone, even though I still didn't have to pee. Henry was still peeing for us both, pulling over to find a "little girls' room" every hundred klicks or so.

Both of Homer's eyes—the big brown and the beady, black—were still closed tight. The Cupper™ on her head was still getting bigger, and was still warm to the touch. "CARRY ON," said the Finder.

South and east of Toledo, just after sliding through an EzGo, I heard the familiar *pop-pop-pop* against the back of the van.

This time Henry was awake, driving. "It's back?"

"What?"

"You know what. The bug."

I said I guessed it was. Henry drove on, counting on me to get rid of it later.

It was late afternoon, getting dark, before I saw the

orange and blue flags in the distance. We were in the outer suburbs of Chicago. I could see towers on the horizon like broken teeth, dim in the cold and growing colder haze. The flee market was in the parking lot of a stadium right on the Indiana line.

Henry was getting cramps again. I gave her the next-to-last pill, and while she went to find the "little girls' room" in the stadium, I pulled Homer in her wagon through the tables. The vendors eyed us meanly, their tables almost bare. I barely slowed for pharms (no HalfLife™ anyway) and went straight to the center of the star.

The no-query was a Black man in coveralls, wearing a blue and orange badge. I didn't offer him a blue. He picked a red out of the stack of whites and reds in my hand and gave me twenty-five, which I figured was half its value.

It seemed a fortune. I spent ten on bush meat and rushed back to Henry—with fifteen still in hand. She was less excited than I was. "The more we get for them, the less eager we should be to get rid of them," she said, rather mysteriously, I thought, since it contradicted her previous position.

There was no wood for a fire so we ate the bush meat cold. Homer nosed it and growled, eyes still closed, but wouldn't eat.

After supper Henry took the fifteen to look for HalfLife™, thinking she might have better luck. She came back with a bottle of HeyGoodLookin' but no pills. "How many are left?" she asked gloomily.

I showed her. One. "For in the morning."

I explored the entire underside of the van before I found the bug, nestled under the transmission. When I peeled it off I felt a slight shock, so slight I thought it might have been my imagination. It wasn't, though. Its little eye was flashing malevolently (I thought). They learn, though they learn slowly, and I was going to have to use gloves next time.

But there wouldn't be a next time. This time I had a plan. I went back to the flee market, which was just closing (it was almost midnight) and bought a mason jar with a screw-top lid.

I put the bug into the jar and screwed the lid on tight.

I crossed the parking lot to the stadium and found the "little boys' room." It had an old-fashioned water toilet. I put the jar in the tank and slid the lid over it; it was heavy and it made a satisfying heavy sound, like the lid of a tomb closing.

Henry was already asleep when I got back to the van. I rolled up beside her and fell asleep listening to Homer snore. When I woke up it was dawn, or at least dawn's pink precursor. The light on the plains is very dramatic, lighting up half the world at a time. It's like being inside an egg.

Bob was as stiff as a pencil. It took both of us to drag his body between the front seats to start the van. "You drive," Henry said; she was already getting a cramp. We were down to the bottom of the bottle. I split the last pill and gave her half.

"TAKE I-80 HEADING WEST," said the Finder. While Henry sat with her eyes closed, waiting for the HalfLife™ to kick in, I "drove," wondering how much farther we would have to go before we reached the end of Finder Nine, whatever that might be. And indeed, today was the day we were going to find out. But first . . .

Ohio had been big, and Indiana bigger, but Illinois was biggest of all: all sky, and underneath it, corn and beans. The Earth was sunlit and peaceful, but the air was filled with marching storms, strutting across the sky, from west to east. I-80 led straight west, across endless fields of corn stubble, some of it still being worked by immense robot gleaners which crossed the interstate through tunnels, often bunching up and jerking like animals impatient to get at the corn they wanted.

Every hour or so we stopped for a "little girls' room." Other than that, Henry had nothing to say. She drove, or watched through the windshield while I "drove," her bluebird sweater gray, her lips settled into what looked like a permanent frown.

She was barely speaking to me. I didn't care. I was more interested in Homer, who seemed to be getting better and better instead of worse. She lay quietly in the Radio Flyer™ with the Cupper™ on her head, now perfectly a part of her. It even had grown yellow fur, so that it looked as if she had a bigger head. I reached back and patted her. She seemed peaceful, dreaming as her little wagon bumped from side to side. I dreamed, too, as I "drove." I began to think that we might actually make Finder Nine. I even allowed myself to dream of what I would do when we got there. It would be a casino. We would cash in our remaining chips for big money, and gamble with some of the rest. I would get my record back, slip it into the jacket, and—

My imagination always gave out at that point. "CARRY ON," said the Finder, but I couldn't. The dream gave out and only the highway continued on.

I was at the wheel in the late afternoon, when I heard a *pop-pop-popp*ing sound at the back of the van. I was so convinced that we had lost the bug that at first I thought it was a stone thrown up by the tires.

But Henry knew better. "Your little friend is back," she said. I shrugged, offended by her attitude and alarmed—and I admit it, a little flattered—by the bug's persistence.

Henry was driving when we saw the orange and yellow flags that meant we were approaching the state line and the flee markets. She started to slot left, but I said, "Wait!" Beyond the flags I could see the towers of a bridge.

"Let's keep going," I said. "We should be coming to the Mississippi."

She looked at me like, so what?

"There may be a casino. Why bother with a no-query and bush meat, when with any luck we could get real money for our chips? And maybe even real food for our money!"

She looked at me like, okay.

The Finder agreed: "STAY ON I-80 ACROSS THE MISSISSIPPI RIVER BRIDGE."

"I hope you're right," said Henry, as I slotted back into a faster lane just in time to ramp up onto the bridge.

I was right.

The Mississippi at Rock Island, with its attendant flood-plains, natural and artificial, is almost three miles wide. On the far bank was a giant sign: a grandmotherly woman beck-oning with a huge finger. GOLDEN YEARS CASINO, EXIT ONE, EZ OFF, EZ ON.

The golden letters flickered on and off as the finger crooked and straightened, crooked and straightened.

"Jackpot!" I said.

But Henry was pointing at a smaller sign: VIEW POINT, indi-cating a half-moon-shaped pull-out in the precise center of the bridge. "Pull over," she said.

I slotted right. "What's this about?" I asked.

"Your little friend."

"I don't know why you persist in calling it 'my little friend'!" I said as I let the van stop next to the rail. "It's fol-lowing the van, not me."

"It's your Bureau," she said, which was ridiculous. We weren't even sure it was a Bureau bug. And it was hardly my Bureau anymore, not unless I caught up with the album by the end of the month.

I was about to tell her all this but she was already out of the van, kneeling, reaching up under the side.

"Maybe it had a geography algorithm," she said, in her librarian voice. "Maybe if we get rid of the bug here, before crossing the Mississippi, it won't follow us into the West."

Not likely, but . . .

"Let me do it," I said. "I know where to find it. Plus, it'll shock you."

Bob's shoeless feet were sticking out of the rolled-up rug. I pulled off one of his socks to use as a glove and crawled under the van, on the cold concrete of the bridge. I found the bug perched on a brake caliper. I touched it gingerly, even through the sock, but to my surprise it didn't shock me at all.

Instead, it sent a warm, pleasant tingling through my fingertips.

"Give it here," Henry said.

I handed it to her and crawled out from under the van. By
the time I got to my feet, she had already dropped a rock into
the sock and was about to drop rock, sock, and bug over the
rail.

"Wait!" I said.

"Huh?" But she waited.

"Need to tie it," I lied. Actually I just wanted one last
look. Was I imagining things, or was its little red eye bright
with terror, panic, longing?

I tied a knot in the sock and handed it back to Henry.

She dropped it over the rail. It fell for what seemed a long
time. Then it hit the water and sank.

"So long!" Henry said with either a grin or a grimace. It
was getting dark but I thought (or imagined) I could see the
dim outline of a bluebird on her sweater as we climbed back
into the van.

"You drive," she said.

"CARRY ON," said the Finder, but I had a plan: I took Exit
One instead, switchbacking up the bluff to a parking lot
filled with buses, under the giant flickering crooked finger we
had seen from across the river.

"Let's cash in our chips," I said. "Let's stay in a mohotel.
Let's eat in a restaurant."

The casino was filled with milling, eating, gabbing, lever-
pulling seniors, all in light blue, white, and pink. Old folks
hate black, which suggests, one supposes, the grave. While
Henry went to find the "little girls' room," I edged through
the crowd looking for the cashier. On my way, I scoped out
the chips the old folks were using. They all said UIC.

The room smelled of incense and ozone; the light was elec-
tric, all neon and halogen; the sound was a surflike crashing
of levers and bells, over the dull slip and slack of plastic

chips. I counted mine in my pocket. Seven left—three white, two red, and two blue.

There was a line at the cashier's cage. The attendant, behind the bars, wore a cowboy hat, just like Indian Bob back in Jersey. I handed him my little stack of chips, and without hesitating he counted out three hundreds, three fifties, and four tens. When he pushed the money under the bars, I looked up and saw his face under the wide brim of the hat.

Somehow I wasn't surprised.

He had the same face. The same sad eyes. "Is your name Bob?" I asked.

He nodded and looked past me. "Next!"

"Wait! I need to talk to you!"

"Why?"

"Because," said Henry from behind me. "We have bad news. It's about your brother, if your name is Bob."

"Oh dear," he said. "Wait till my break."

I gave Henry the money, four-ninety, for safekeeping, and she reached up under her bluebird sweater and hid it somewhere in the unseen machinery of her bra. We munched on shrimp from a free buffet until the cashier's replacement arrived for his twenty-minute, once-a-night (he later told us) break. Then we took him out to the van, looking small and almost sleek, wedged between the large, blunt Illinois and Iowa buses in the lot. Henry unrolled Bob just enough to show his face—and of course, his raised right hand. Was the smell getting worse, or was it just me?

"Oh dear," said Bob, or Robert, or Bobby. "How did he die?"

"You can ask him," Henry said. She already had the spray out, in her hand.

"No, no, no!"

"Where do you want us to put him?" I asked.

"Put him?"

I explained to Robert, to Bobby, to Bob, that we were looking for a place to leave Bob. That we had been told—

"Instructed," said Henry

—to take him to his brother. That we had followed the Finder here, trying to locate Henry's fiance—

"Husband."

—and a certain record album, illegally sold by mistake, which I was trying to get back—

He brightened. "A record album. Is this an Alexandrian thing?"

It was my turn to be coy. "Could be."

"I think I can help you," he said. He stuck out his hand— "Bob"—and explained to me that he was only an employee at the Golden Years. He worked three days and was off three. The record I was looking for was at his place. If we waited until morning, when he got off, he would take us there.

Bob, too.

It sounded like a good deal to me. Henry, too.

While Henry went back into the casino with Bob, to find the "little girls' room" (she said), I lay down in the back of the van between Bob and Homer. The night was oddly warm. Homer's head felt warm and furry, not hot and slick like before. Was the Cupper ™ growing fur? I wondered, stroking it while she snored and I circled that dot of darkness that is sleep, that tiny black hole that eats past present and future.

When I woke up, it was daylight and Henry was still gone. I was alone in the van with Bob and Homer. It was impossible to tell what time it was. The Golden Years Casino sign was flickering, casting an eerie light over the parking lot, in which the huge buses looked like beached whales, all in a line.

And I had the strangest feeling, which it took me a while to recognize, or rather, remember. I had to pee.

Chapter 30

What about nonfiction? What about fiction disguised as nonfiction? What about nonfiction disguised as fiction? What about essays on fiction, criticism, journalism? What about authors who wrote in one mode and dabbled in another?

It seemed, at first, anyway, that literature called for different procedures than the visual arts, since books were being produced at a greater volume than ever. There was more urgency to the matter. Add to that the fact that there were (or appeared to be, at least) more different types of books than paintings. The first task was to distinguish between the books that were part of the historical legacy, and those that were entertainment or art only. It was decided that only fiction and poetry were to be deleted. Since fiction of earlier times was often part of the historical record of society as well as of fiction itself, it was decided that only authors born after 1900 were to be eligible for deletion, and only their eligible works of fiction and/or poetry. Thus Mark Twain and F. Scott Fitzgerald joined Shakespeare and Sir Walter Scott in literature's permanent Hall of Fame, and Salinger and Smiley were left to take their chances with the rest. But did not old paintings and drawings also have historical value in addition to and sometimes even above and beyond their artistic value? In other words, once again, what about Michelangelo? Or Rubens or Cezanne? The answer had already presented itself in literature, and thus it was that Monet joined Michelangelo among the immortals, while Pollock and Warhol did not. All these deliberations took days. The meetings began *promptly at nine a.m. after a quick buffet breakfast, and lasted until six, with a one hour buffet lunch. The evenings were restricted to the hotel, which had a hot tub and a small pool, a weight room, a bar, and a considerable book and film library. Damaris never consorted privately with the others; her screen was dimmed after the proceedings every day. Indeed the Round Table members rarely interacted with one another. It was as if their personalities and opinions were dimmed when they were apart.*

Poets, like novelists, were to be deleted all at once. Poets born before 1900 were to be spared. Drama was easily disposed of, since a play, like a novel, was gone with its author. Memoirs, however candid, were considered fiction, while history, however fanciful, was considered fact, leading some to observe that it was the personal and not the fictional that elevated writing to literature. And dance? Each dance was left to die on its own, along with the recorded performances of stand-up and imitation.

Music and film were left. Film was easy, since the works were in all cases produced by a team or a group. It was no longer sufficient (or necessary) to delete individuals; rather, it was the film itself that was struck from the public record. What if the film was a remake, such as Psycho3 *or* Prettier Woman*? A remake, it was agreed, was a separate film. And the Movie Star, the highest paid, pre-eminent artist of the twentieth century, lasted only as long as her (or his) films.*

Music presented similar problems without the easy solution. The work and the artist had a maddeningly complex relationship here, musicians often performing the work of other musicians with the help of other musicians still. What about the group, such as the Beatles; was it to be deleted at once, or die a slow death as its members were deleted? What about the leader, like Miles Davis, who formed and reformed groups, often with others who later formed groups of their own? What about the performer and composer who were one and the same, like Hank Williams or Thelonious Monk? Did the performer outlive the composer, or did both enter oblivion at once? What about folk music? Easy in a sense, since it was like folk art, except that it was always performed and often rewritten. Suppose recorded music were deleted piece by piece, like film. Should a great artist (Miles Davis was again the example) be subjected to the same slow, piecemeal death as a Movie Star like Tom Hanks? To add to the difficulty, the cut-off date which had rescued both literature and art from so many difficulties was meaningless, since no recording was done before 1900. What about 2000, then? After that the album or collection became mostly a thing of the past, most music being digital on-demand. What about making everything produced between 1900 and 2000 deletable? It was Mr. Bill who made this suggestion, breaking with his "observer" stance (or rather, as it turned out, pose). There were immortals in literature and art, if only by chronological default. What if in music, only "immortals" were deleted? At this, several members of the Round Table fell silent, including Damaris. Others grew more animated. What if a list were compiled of the, say, one thousand most influential musicians of the twentieth century—the century in question, the century in which music became both more inclusive (adding jazz and rock), more serious (financially and critically) and more permanent, through recording. These "nonimmortals" would be deleted one by one. This proposal cast a gloom over parts of the Round Table while animating others. "What about musicians like Hank Williams or Thelonious Monk," Damaris said, growing more and more agitated. "Are they to be murdered twice?"

"The issue is not murder," said Mr. Bill.

"It feels like murder," said Damaris, pacing her tiny cell, which looked even tinier on the tiny screen. "This is bothering me. I'm beginning to realize the enormity of what we are

proposing. This is only partly about works. It is ultimately about . . ."

"It's about cleansing the canon," said Mr. Bill. *His normal nerdy harmless look was gone. He was getting red in the face. He reached over to dim her screen.*

Someone suggested a break for lunch.

Chapter 31

I had to pee! Eagerly, I got out of the van.

It was dawn, or dawn's pink next-door neighbor, and I walked to the edge of the lot and stood between two buses, both from Illinois, and peed down a steep clay bank, and it felt great. It felt like coming home. Did this mean I was healed? I dropped my sky blue, one-stripe pants and checked my leg and saw that the Cupper™ was gone, except for a raised spot, like an old burn scar on my thigh. I could scratch it; it was part of me.

Homer was still snoring when I got back to the van. Was she also healed? The Cupper™ on her head no longer looked as if it could be peeled off. It looked like a fur hat. It was still warm to the touch, though, and her eyes were still closed.

And where was Henry? Still in the casino. Her rug was rolled up as if she had never slept in it. I had a bad feeling as I went inside to look for her. The Golden Years was as busy now, at dawn, as it had been the previous evening. The seniors seemed tireless, pulling the levers as if they were powering a dynamo (which, it turns out, they were; but I'm getting ahead of myself).

I found Henry sitting glumly at a table staring at a small pile of chips. Three whites.

"Chips!?" I said. "Where'd you get these? What happened to our money?" She looked up at me, glassy-eyed, and I knew the worst.

It was 7:57. The Indian, Bob, cashed us in for three tens, all of which I kept. At 8:00 he gave his keys to his replacement (an elderly woman), filled a plastic bag with freshwater farm shrimp and cocktail tomatoes from the buffet, and followed Henry and me out to the van.

Henry went to sleep in the back, rolled up in the rug. She had stayed up all night and gambled away all our money. "You shouldn't have given her the chips," I said to Bob, as he started the van for me. He and our Bob (and all the Bobs) had the same fingerprints.

"I'm a cashier," he said, "not a financial adviser. Not a social worker. If I didn't give chips to anybody I thought would lose, the place would go out of business and I would be out of a job."

I couldn't argue with that. But the fact was, we were almost broke—for real, this time. "FOLLOW THE INTERSTATE WEST," said the Finder, and so I did. We didn't need the Finder (I assumed it was taking us to Indian Bob's) but Bob seemed to find it amusing. We drove straight across the low rolling hills toward the always receding horizon. There were no more flee markets, now that we were west of the Mississippi, but it didn't matter anyway. We were out of chips and out of money, too, except for my pathetic three tens.

While I "drove," Bob talked.

"I'm Bob 26," he said. "But my friends just call me Bob. The Years is run by a consortium from Denmark. They run most of the Indian gambling operations, though we don't advertise that. We work as cashiers, some of us."

"We?"

"The Bobs," he said. "The Indian Bobs." He explained that he was one of seventy-seven Robert Lightfoots that (or rather, who) had been cloned in an attempt to preserve the full-blooded Native American population. "It was an experiment," he said, "that went awry. Is that the word, awry? Anyway, a baker's dozen of the Bobs died in the tank before we were even 'born.' The rest of us are all the same age— what would you guess?"

This is always a tricky business, even with normal people. I usually guess low and then subtract. He looked about forty-five, so I said, "Thirty-five."

He looked as pleased as a cat with a canary. "Sixty-one and a half."

"Our Bob, too?"

"We're all the same age," Bob said. "It was all done in a lab in Oklahoma, top secret. So when the funding was cut, after only three years, there was no way to get it renewed, or is the word revived? Anyway, it meant no girls."

"Girls?"

"Females. Squaws, dames, you know. The plan was to clone up seventy-seven matching females, so we could start a second generation. But the Republicans came in and the funding was withdrawn and the project was dropped and the females were never made. We never got any education, either, any of us. That's why so many Bobs went into boot-legging."

I started to warn him that he couldn't talk about bootleg-ging, but then I remembered that I was on Modified Duty, whatever that meant. So I kept my mouth shut, and "drove" and listened while he explained that the Bobs used the casi-nos as drops for bootleg goods. He had noticed a record in a box of books and CDs that had been dropped at his place a few days ago. Hopefully it hadn't been picked up yet.

"Hopefully," I said. "It's very valuable and I have to get it back." I pointed at the Hank Williams album cover wedged between the two front seats.

"I see," he said. He hadn't noticed it before. "So that explains the Dusty Springfield."

"CARRY ON," said the Finder.

"Dusty who?"

"We use Dusty Springfield album covers on the most valu-able, the most priciest, the rarest. The ones that go straight to Vegas. It's camouflage."

"Vegas?"

"The Alexandrians," he said. "They are the only ones who can afford the really rare, pricey stuff."

"Did you hear that, Henry?" I asked over the back of the seat. "We're going to Vegas. Just like I thought."

But Henry wasn't listening. She was snoring away with Homer. And I was wondering why Bob was telling me all this. He had apparently decided he could trust us, but why?

Nothing looked Western. I had always thought that the Mississippi marked the beginning of the West, but so far—fifty, then a hundred kilometers into Iowa—everything in every direction was midwestern. Corn and beans and big trees clustered around the houses, like huge friendly dogs.

Indian Bob rattled on about everything, even about rattling on. "My brothers tell me I talk a lot," he said. "Let me know if it bothers you." I told him it didn't. It was nice to have somebody to talk to, or listen to, anyway. Usually Henry was silent, even when she was awake. I watched her in the rearview mirror, waking up. She opened her eyes. She checked under her sweater (probably wondering if losing our money had been a dream) and closed her eyes again. It was no dream!

"CARRY ON," said the Finder.

Listening to Bob as I "drove," I learned that the reason the casino sign flickered was that it ran on electricity generated by the machines themselves. "Old folks pulling the levers," Bob said. "They light the sign and pull more old folks in. There's even a little surplus, sold to the grid. We may be using it now. What year van is this?"

I told him I had no idea. "It was Bob's."

"No it wasn't," said Henry. She was awake. I could tell by her voice she was having a cramp. "Time for my pill," she said, holding her hand between the two front seats.

I gave her the last of Homer's HalfLife™.

"Thanks," she said, swallowing the pill without a chaser. "This van was Bob's brother's. In Jersey. I assume you are related?"

I tuned out while Bob explained about the cloning, the seventy-seven Indian Bobs.

"Wow," said Henry. "That's kind of a conversation stopper."

"Everything's a conversation stopper with you," I said.

"What do you mean by that?"

"Please!" said Bob. "Our exit is up ahead, in just a mile or two."

As if on cue, the Finder chimed in: "TAKE EXIT SEVEN, THREE KILOMETERS."

"I hope there's a 'little girls' room,'" said Henry. "I have to powder my nose."

"Me, too," I said, enjoying her shocked look.

"What do you mean!?"

"Just what I said," I said.

"EXIT LEFT ON COUNTY ROAD 12 NORTH," said the Finder.

"That's us," said Bob. "Cottonwood Creek Road."

Cottonwood! That sounded Western. But the road still looked midwestern, heading straight across rolling fields of corn, corn, corn. About a mile up the road, the Finder and Bob both identified a low concrete block building under a faded billboard

INDIAN BOB'S
STEAKS AND SLOTS

"PULL INTO THE LOT," said the Finder. "THIS ENDS SEARCH UNIT NINE. PRESS ESCAPE TO EXIT GEO SEARCH. PRESS MENU FOR A NEW SEARCH."

I pulled in, pressed escape, and so forth, while Bob gathered his plastic bag of white shirts and said, "Follow me." The building was boarded up. We slipped behind a loose plywood 4 × 8 into a dusty darkness that smelled like french fries and rats.

I even heard a scurrying.

"They're gone," said Bob. My eyes gradually grew accustomed to the dark and I saw him standing by an old pool table. "They're usually left here by one Bob and picked up by another. I have nothing to do with it. I just happened to notice the record album, like I said."

"So where is the next Bob's?" Henry asked. She was pleased, I could tell. She wanted to keep heading west. I was disappointed. I wanted to get the record and go home before my job was lost forever.

"Beats me," Bob said. "Need to know, you know. Try the Finder. It'll send you to the next one, like an Indian pony."

"So where is the 'little girls' room'?"

While Henry used the "little girls' room," I ducked outside to pee behind a cottonwood. It was still a novelty. It felt good. Even though I was disappointed that the album was gone, I was still hopeful. At least I knew I was on its trail.

Henry and Bob slipped out the crack that was a door. "You can stay the night," said Bob. "You can sleep inside with me if you want to, but you'll be more comfortable outside, in the van, I think." I agreed. I couldn't stand the musty smell of the old casino and steak house. Not to mention the rats.

I gathered wood for a fire while Henry unwrapped the shrimp and rolls. It was like playing house. Bob joined us for dinner. Afterwards, he found a half bottle of HeyGood-Lookin' in the casino, and we passed it back and forth across the fire. After a few drinks, Henry asked Bob if he wanted "a few last words" with our Bob. A whiskey idea if there ever was one. But I kept my mouth shut while they opened Bob's.

"Oh no!" he said. "Am I dead?" It seems like people who are dead are always rediscovering it. And hating it.

"Bob, it's me, Henry!"

"Henry who?"

"You lied to me, didn't you? You told me you were an Alexandrian. You said you talked to Panama every week."

Indian Bob was shocked. "He told you he was an Alexandrian?"

"I'm sorry! My hands are cold!"

Henry blew on his hands, which were locked together, and put them up under her bluebird sweater. I was surprised to find that I was a little jealous.

"Here's your brother, Bob," she said. "You want to talk to him?"

"Bob? Where are we?"

"Iowa," Bob told him.

"Really? It's so dark!"

"It's night," said Henry.

"And you're dead," I said.

"Oh no!" he said. "I knew it! Don't leave me here! It's . . . cold."

His mouth closed. His eyes opened. Henry pulled his hands out from under her sweater and rolled him back up in his rug.

"Didn't you want to ask him something?" she asked Bob.

He shook his head. "I just wanted to see how it worked. I can't believe he told you he was an Alexandrian."

Henry went to sleep and Bob and I finished the whiskey. I was feeling mellow, so I asked, "Where do you want to bury Bob? I'll help you in the morning."

"No, no, no," Bob said. "Not here. You have to take him on."

"To the next Indian Bob's? What if it's closed down, too?"

"To the cemetery," he said. "All the Bobs are buried in one cemetery. It's part of the deal. We don't get an education, or a girl, or a decent job, but we get a burial plot. I'll be buried there myself someday."

"Where?"

"I don't really know," he said, passing me the bottle. "Don't really want to know, if you know what I mean. I'm sure it's on the Finder. Try the last number, whatever it is. Me, I'm going to bed."

There was one drink left. I finished the whiskey and went to sleep in the van next to Henry. It was a warm night but my hands were cold. I put them up under her bluebird sweater but she batted them away, sleepily.

Something woke me later. I thought it was a noise. Then I realized it was a silence.

Homer had quit snoring. I reached up and felt her nose and it was cold. Was she feeling better? The Cupper™ was furry and warm, like a hat. I had to pee. Did she have to pee?

I stepped outside the van. It was as bright as day. The moon had risen, and in the past few days since I had seen it (in Staten Island; it seemed a lifetime ago) it had gotten almost full. The streak was so bright that I had to squint to look at it. They say something is written there but I can never read it. Twenty years ago a rocket filled with robots was sent up to smooth an area on the moon for a print ad. By the time it was finished the company had failed and the robots had (supposedly) died. Now all that is left is the streak, like a bright Band-Aid™ across the face of the stony little planet.

I stepped into the shadows to pee. Peeing is a luxurious and sensuous event when you've missed it awhile. I was just zipping up when I felt something hit my hand.

I looked around. Had someone thrown a rock? Who? Bob? Henry?

Then I saw the glittering red eye on the ground at my feet.

The bug! It had found us again. But this time it had specifically found me, and not the van, which was only a few feet away, in the darkness.

I picked it up carefully—but instead of stinging me it felt

warm, and tingly. I didn't want to let go. It had tracked us across the Midwest, almost to the West, off the interstate and down into this grove of cottonwoods. I couldn't imagine how it had gotten out of the sock. Maybe it had washed up on a snag; maybe a boy, fishing, had pulled it from the water and set it free, a Huck Finn. I could imagine him finding it, thinking it was a lure; I could imagine his surprise as it flew away.

I wondered if it gave his fingers the same tingly glow. It felt so good I didn't want to let it go. But I had things to do, places to go. I found a mason jar in the junk by the front of the casino. I put the bug in the jar and screwed the lid on tight.

Then tighter. Then tighter still.

I was looking for a shovel when I got a better idea. There was a falling-down barbed-wire fence by the cottonwoods, where the van was parked. I worked a cedar post loose and pulled it up, then dropped the jar down into the hole. Was it my imagination, or was the little red eye pleading with me as I pushed the post back into place? All this in the blinding light of the full moon.

I propped my feet on the dash and went to sleep in the driver's seat.

The next morning when I woke up, Henry was leaning across me, reaching between my legs, surfing through the Finder.

"They all say go east, except for two. Eleven and twenty. They both say the same thing, Interstate 80 west."

"Let's try twenty," I said (the last one). Again, I had to pee. Again, Homer didn't. Her eyes were still closed. But her breathing was regular, her nose was cold. The Cupper™ was covered with golden fur, making her look like a mutt with a thoroughbred head.

Indian Bob was still asleep so we had to start the van with our Bob, who was getting stiffer and stiffer. I held him rolled

up in the rug in my arms while Henry guided his outstretched, stiffened finger into the ignition pad. "Why don't
we just cut it off?" I asked.

Henry gave me a look. "His hand? Are you serious?"

I was. "He'll never know."

"I will," she said, and that was that.

Indian Bob was waiting by the door of the Casino and
Steak House as we pulled out. Henry asked him if he wanted
a last look at Bob. "No, no, no," he said.

"TAKE COUNTRY ROAD TWELVE SOUTH," said the Finder.
"TAKE INTERSTATE 80 WEST." Henry "drove," slotting us into
a fast lane train of trucks, while I dozed, worn out from my
moonlight rambling and digging. When I woke up we were
in Nebraska. The state started as an Illinois or an Iowa:
rolling fields, more flat than rolling. Trees in the fencerows.
Barns, sheds, and houses in the trees. Then the land got
higher and drier.

We were in a river valley, the Platte, thick with cottonwoods and midwestern barns. But on the horizon, to the
north, I could see high dunes like Arabia. They were pressing
in on both sides, as if eager to devour us and everything
moist.

The West. We were not yet in it, but we were rubbing up
against it. I looked at the album cover, the picture of Hank
Williams in his cowboy hat getting into (or out of) his Cadillac. What did the West have to do with the South, and what
did any of it have to do with me?

I was interrupted in thinking these thoughts by a strange
gravelly noise. I turned around and looked into the back of
the van. Bob's rug had unrolled just enough to show one
hideous, dessicated, shrunken cheek. Homer's Radio Flyer™
was rocking gently, an inch forward, an inch back. All that
was normal.

What was unusual, what was miraculous and astonishing
and wonderful, was that Homer had both eyes open. Both
were beautiful, big brown eyes, looking right at me—

"Homer!" I said.

"Something smells good," she answered in a low, gravelly voice.

"Oh no," Henry groaned.

I didn't know what to groan, or say, or even think. We had a talking dog.

Chapter 32

That was to be the end of the Round Table. When the group came back from lunch (always a silent and solitary business, as everyone was anxious to avoid compromising friendships) Damaris's screen was dimmed. Mr. Bill said that Damaris had withdrawn. She felt that the work was done and was anxious to begin her prison sentence. She had sent a statement, which he read. It thanked everyone for their work and declared the project a success, a validation of the sacrifices she and the other Alexandrians had made. Even though that sounded unlikely (to some) the group accepted it. What choice did they have?

Ironically or perhaps happily, Mr. Bill went on to say, this was to be the last session anyway. The few who were surprised by this checked their palm calendars and nodded in agreement, some reluctant, most not. The unity was gone, and with it, the good feeling. The last afternoon was devoted to a discussion of the proposal to delete only the most successful musicians of the twentieth century. The argument that this was too subjective was met with the answer that music was the least subjective of the arts, since it was all quantifiable through sales. Wouldn't that make Alanis Morissette more important than, say, Gerry Mulligan? No. The one thousand cut-off would provide a big enough pool to include all on an equal basis. When a musician's recordings were deleted, the work as sidemen on other works could either be left, nonattributed, or be filled in with generic digital. The compositions would enter public domain and not be deleted (like books or

*films). It was objected that this was an entirely different, and
even opposite, system from the one used in literature, where
the giants were in fact immortalized. The objection was not
answered. Mr. Bill thanked everyone, reminding them that
the purpose of the Round Table was not to provide working
solutions but only to suggest directions. That work was
done. In their rooms that night, everyone found an envelope
containing a plane ticket and a check for a million dollars.
Three weeks and four days later the hotel was demolished for
a new north-south runway.*

Chapter 33

The West begins not at the Mississippi, or even in Iowa, but somewhere in the middle of Nebraska, along a line that runs from Canada down to Mexico, roughly along the ninety-eighth parallel. This line is nowhere as visible as a river or as sudden as an escarpment, but it is everywhere apparent as a sort of drift, as gradual but as inexorable as a sunrise, from the tree-filled draws of the outer Midwest to the broken, dry land of the true West.

The sky is bigger; brighter, too.

"CARRY ON," said the van, as we drove deeper into the West, or out of the everything else that the West is not. We switched, and Henry dozed while I drove. I found the emptiness exhilarating. The dawn of the West—which is what Nebraska was, and always will be to me—brought a sense of hope: *Maybe things will all work out after all.* I can see now that it was a hope that defied both experience and expectation; but isn't that what hope is all about?

And besides, things were already changing for the better. All I had to do to be reminded of that was look in the rearview mirror and see Homer's big, brown eyes, both open now, gazing back at me the same way they always had.

Almost the same, anyway.

"Something smells good," she said again in her deep, gravelly drawl.

"Looks like we have a talking dog," said Henry, again, without opening her eyes.

I was glad to have Homer back, but less than thrilled about the talking part. One of the nice things about dogs (not to conflate Homer with all dogs, though all dogs are, in their way, alike) is that we can talk to them and they never answer. But now another never was over.

"What do you think it means?" I asked Henry.

"Beats me," she said, without opening her eyes. "Ask her."

I tried. "Homer!" I said. "What's the deal? What happened? How'd you learn to talk? Does it have something, anything, to do with the Cupper™?"

"Something smells weird," she said.

"CARRY ON," said the Finder.

On I carried. Nebraska was wide and dry and flat, and getting wider and drier and flatter as we sped west, wedged in a convoy of wire-trucks. The interstate sliced through a gray expanse of dying grass with an occasional dune poking through, stretching as far as the eye could see. No trees anywhere. No towns. Nothing but sky and grass and an occasional blister of sand—or a windmill, turning relentlessly in the relentless prairie wind.

Contrails of jets in their safety formations of three streaked across the slate gray sky. The West! Hank Williams looked at me from under his hat, from the door of his Caddy. What treasures, what secrets, did the West contain, after all? Or was it all an illusion, like so much of life, so far, had been?

Henry was hungry so we spent one of our two tens on a discount carry-out lunch of bush meat at an All Rest just past Platte City. Henry ate only a few bites, then ran for the bathroom. "Upset stomach?" I asked, when she got back to the van.

It was worse than that. "Cramps. I never got my morning pill. And now I won't get my afternoon either."

I drove faster, slotting us into the truck lane, as if that would make up somehow for the HalfLife™ we didn't have, and had no way to find now that we were in the West, where there were no flee markets and no no-queries. "CARRY ON," said the Finder. So on I carried, deeper into the unknown but not unfamiliar West.

I drove all night. We passed through one EzGo, marking the Wyoming line. Next would be Nevada, I knew (even without a map) from Academy. Henry moaned and groaned in her sleep, asking first for Panama, then for Bob. Homer kept me company, in her way, half sleeping, but with one big brown eye on me in the rearview.

I decided to try again. "How long have you been able to talk?" I asked.

"Something smells wrong," she said.

"That's just the way it seems," I said. "I never meant to steal the Williams. Just to listen to it. It was stolen from me, and I'm trying to recover it."

The sun went down but the moon was high, and I turned off the lights and drove by the light of the streak for a hundred miles, just for fun. There was something about the West, all that emptiness, that made me want to drive, drive, drive, as though I were disappearing.

Disappearing.

Another EzGo had to be Nevada. When I looked back, Henry was rolled up with Bob in the rug, and Homer was snoring away, both eyes closed.

The moon was going down. I slotted over to a deserted rest area to stretch my legs and pee. There was the windowless shell of a gas station, a few islands where gas-o-line pumps had been, and a couple of junked pickups, facing the highway like antelopes. I got out and I was the only living person in a hundred miles in every direction. There was no wind, no trucks passing, no lights in any direction. Then I made the mistake of looking up. The stars were coming out, one by one at first, then in clusters and clumps of four and ten, then in streaks and bands of a hundred, a thousand. Soon the whole sky would be ablaze . . .

I was zipping up my pants when I felt something hit my hand. I looked down and there, staring up from the pavement, was the unblinking red eye of the bug.

I almost stepped on it. But I didn't. I picked it up, and instead of a sting, I felt an indescribably pleasant tingle.

I bounced it in my fingertips and the palm of my hand. The tingle was almost intimate. I felt a strange comradeship with the bug, in the center of all this emptiness. We were, in a way, two of a kind: both heading somewhere else. Neither of us knowing where, or why.

One of the junked pickups was a midcentury Chevrolet with click-open doors and a bench seat. I slid into the driver's seat. The steering wheel spun easily; the front end was up on blocks. Through the windshield I could see snow-covered mountains, ghostly as clouds.

I put the bug into the glove compartment and clicked it shut. Then I got back into the van and drove on, west.

Henry woke up groaning, again, but I had no more pills to give her. We did find some coffee, in a pull-aside machine that made us listen to a minute of ads. I took Homer for a "walk" in her wagon but she showed no desire to "do her business" so I gave it up. Her Cupper™ hadn't turned into scar tissue, like mine. Instead it perched on her head like a mushroom shaped hat, still orange, still hot. I suspected that it had something to do with her newfound ability to talk.

"I'll drive," said Henry. She liked to do her driving in the morning. I realized I hadn't seen her bluebirds in several days. They had disappeared from her sweater altogether—it was gray on gray.

"I-80 WEST," said the Finder, and Henry slotted us into the empty truck lane. There were no exits, no services. Twice we passed cloverleafs for north-south interstates, one of them streaming with trucks and the other empty. But there was no access to the world, or nonworld, of rock and sand and sagebrush.

The road was straight as an arrow toward the intriguing snowy mountains on the horizon. I never got to see them up close, though. My eyelids got heavier and heavier. I had driven all night, and now I crawled into the back with Bob and Homer and slept all day.

When I woke up it was midafternoon and the mountains were gone. Had we passed over them? Gone around them? Henry was no help. "I've been watching the road," she said. "Not the scenery. You want to drive awhile?"

T AKE THE NEXT EXIT SOUTH," said the Finder, in my dream. "COMING IN TWO KILOMETERS."

I jerked and sat up. I had been dozing. I hit repeat.

"TAKE THIS NEXT EXIT SOUTH," the Finder said again, in real life. "COMING IN ONE KILOMETER."

No road number? The exit was a cloverleaf, but the highway it connected with looked abandoned. It was an interstate, or at least a four lane, but sand was drifted over it and sagebrush grew out of big cracks in the concrete. I entered slowly and the yellow light on the dash told me I was off the grid. I had to steer. The road led due south toward a range of hills that looked like a pile of bones.

"CARRY ON," said the Finder.

"Something smells spooky," said Homer, who was now awake.

I had to steer. I had to pay close attention to make sure we didn't run off the road, into the sand and rocks. I swerved to miss a tumbling tumbleweed. I knew what they were from Zane Grey.

"Where are we?" Henry sat up, groaned, and slid into the front seat next to me.

"Finder nine, I guess," I said. "Almost there, I hope."

"Almost where?" she said, looking around. "This is nowhere. We could die out here."

"Doubtful," I said. But I was bluffing. The van, which sup-

THE PICKUP ARTIST   171

posedly had a range of a hundred kilometers off the grid, was already slowing down. The yellow battery light was turning red. Perhaps it was the swerving. The sand was drifted up onto the road in crescents half as high as a man. I had to weave in and out, around them. Sometimes the wheels tipped up, onto the sand.

"There!" Henry said. In the distance, I saw a dot on the highway.

It got bigger and bigger. Closer and closer.

It was a white lectro van. It was traveling north in the southbound lanes, since the northbound lanes were totally covered by sand. But there was plenty of room.

I edged over to let it pass.

It was a van just like ours! On the side it said

INDIAN BOB'S
CASINO & CRAFTS

"Hey!" said Henry. She waved, and the driver waved back as he passed. It was definitely one of the Bobs; I could tell by the hat, the smile, even the wave.

"Wait!" Henry yelled.

I stopped and she got out. She waved and yelled but the van just went on north, into the distance, getting smaller and smaller. "Oooooh! she groaned, bending over double as she got back into our van.

"CARRY ON," said the Finder.

How far had we come off the grid? The van was going slower and slower, down to forty, then thirty kph. We were approaching the bone-shaped mountains and the sun was about to touch the western horizon when I saw the first sign.

INDIAN BOB'S
CASINO AND CRAFTS
HAPPY HUNTING GROUND
EZ OFF, EZ ON

Happy Hunting Ground? Surely that was our destination. Had to be. I wasn't surprised when the Finder chimed in, "TAKE CASINO EXIT."

The next sign said

EXIT HERE FOR
INDIAN BOB'S
AUTHENTIC INDIAN
CASINO & CRAFTS
HAPPY HUNTING GROUND

I saw the big concrete teepee, halfway up a rocky hillside, before I saw the exit. It looked like a missile leaving its silo. The exit was so drifted over with sand that I had to stop and gear the van down to "careful" and let it find its way through. It barely made it up the driveway to the lot.

"DING," said the Finder. "PRESS ESCAPE TO EXIT GEO SEARCH. PRESS MENU FOR NEW CHOICES."

The teepee flapped in the wind and I realized it was not concrete and much smaller than I had thought.

Which meant that the man standing in the doorway wasn't actually a giant.

He tipped his hat and started toward us. He looked a little better than most of the Bobs, until I saw it was because he'd had his teeth replaced with a new and perfect set. After that he looked worse.

"Where's the casino?" I asked.

"Long gone," he said. "Who are you, anyway?"

"Friends," said Henry. She was already out of the van, explaining (or so she thought) herself. "We were sent here by your brother, Indian Bob. We have bad news." She had already opened the sliding door; she was already unrolling our Bob.

His eyes were shriveled like raisins. His lips had shrunk so they no longer covered his teeth. The smell hovered somewhere between sweet and foul.

"Oh dear," said Indian Bob. "Can I ask what happened?"

Henry had a ready answer for that: "You can ask him," she said, holding up the spray can of LastRites™.

"Isn't that stuff addictive?" Indian Bob shook his head. "I'll assume you are his friends if you brought him here in this van."

"Were," I said. "I'm also trying to recover an item, which I mistakenly loaned to him. A very valuable album."

"In a Dusty Springfield jacket?"

"It is supposedly headed for the Alexandrians."

"Sssshhhh!" he said, finger to lips (his version of the Bureau's bootlegging warning?). "You missed it by less than a day." He pointed back down toward the highway.

"You mean the van we passed?"

"Not that one. That was the one that delivered the stuff. Another van took it on." He pointed the other way.

"On to where?" I asked.

"Ssshhhhhh," he said, shaking his head. "Don't need to know. That's the whole idea. Nobody knows more than one stop. Though, it's probably on the Finder."

"This is the last stop on the Finder," I said.

"Then it may be next to last. Or not on there at all. I'm about to have dinner. Would you two care to join me?"

"Something smells good," said Homer.

"A talking dog! Can he handle soup?"

The inside of the teepee was about the size of a mohotel room, and furnished the same, with a blond wood bed, dresser, and TV. There was even a painting on the wall of Paris in the rain.

"Where's your 'little girls' room'?" Henry asked. It was outside, and somewhat less than a "room."

Indian Bob opened four cans of soup (one for Homer, whom I had brought along) and while it heated, fireless, in the can, he told me the story of the Bobs. It varied little from the story the last Bob had told.

"It's a lonely life," said Bob. "You probably think of us as bootleggers, but we were denied an education. Part of the deal with the sale of the casino concession was guaranteed jobs, but who wants a minimum wage job in a casino? We negotiated for something worthless. Sometimes that appears to be the Indian way. More soup?"

"Something smells funny," said Homer.

"A few of the Bobs ended up in the city, like the one you call your Bob, and others drifted back to what was left of the reservations. Some went into the military. There are three Bobs on one aircraft carrier in the Mediterranean, the *Dolphin*. None of us married, though. It's as though we were born with a hole in the heart. You know what I mean? A sort of unfillable emptiness."

"I know what you mean," I said.

"They should have done the girls," said Indian Bob. "It was like we were unfinished from the start. The only one who fell in love was the one you call your Bob."

"Fell in love?" said Henry, who was back from the "little girls' room." "Are you sure?"

"We all tried to keep up with each other," said Indian Bob. "A girl in Brooklyn. An Alexandrian. And now here he is, home at last."

"I didn't know he loved me," said Henry. A few wan bluebirds appeared as she sat teary-eyed over her soup. "I thought he was just doing it for Panama."

"He didn't even know how to find Panama," I reminded her, and the bluebirds went away.

After we had our soup, Henry curled up by the little kerosene stove and went to sleep. The teepee flapped in the wind like a sail. Indian Bob took me up the hill to the cemetery. A faded wooden sign on the gate read:

HAPPY HUNTING GROUND
"HOME OF THE BRAVES"

"We all return here, or try," he said. "Don't ask me why. Maybe it was built in. Maybe it's something we learned. Even the Bob lost at sea (there were originally four on the *Dolphin*) was recovered and brought here. So far there are fourteen filled graves."

The cemetery had a gate but no fence. It was solemn, sad, and neat. And rocky. Seventy-seven graves in seven rows of eleven on a gravelly hillside overlooking the drifted-over interstate. Sixty-three were empty holes. Seventy-seven crosses, all made of white plastic, all marked "Robert Tecumseh Lightfoot" with the birthdate (20—) printed and the death date left blank. Fourteen had the death date pencilled in.

"The graves were all dug at once, by a backhoe," said Indian Bob. "They fill in with blowing sand, and get renewed once a year or so. It was part of the severance deal with the university. Would you like some whiskey?" He reached into an open grave (they were none of them very deep) and pulled up a bottle of HeyGoodLookin'.

Sometimes the wind drops just as the sun does, and an impressive stillness falls over the Earth. It's particularly impressive out West. Bob and I shared a drink, and then another, then he put the bottle back into the grave, next to two short shovels. "For in the morning," he said. "I'll help you with the burial. It's part of our tradition."

You'll help me? I thought. *It's your brother. I'm just along for the ride.* But I didn't say anything. There's a way to do everything, and a way that everything gets done.

As soon as the sun goes down out West, it gets cold.

I slept in the teepee with Indian Bob, Henry, and Homer, arranged around the little kerosene stove like the numbers on a clock. I woke up in the middle of the night to pee. At first I didn't know where I was; then I recognized the flapping of the canvas.

Outside, the wind was howling. I ducked behind the teepee to pee, but because of its shape it provided no protection.

I was zipping up when I felt something hit my hand. At first I thought it was a rock, a limb, a leaf the wind had flung. Then I saw the little red eye looking up from the ground between my feet.

"You."

I put the bug into my pocket; I would deal with it in the morning. Plus I liked the warm tingling feeling it gave me, as I curled up by the hissing kerosene stove.

I dreamed I was on a schooner, sailing across the West. I rescued a sailor from an island shaped like a bone. It was my father, my dad. "Where have you been?" he asked. Or did I only dream I dreamed that dream?

It was morning. The whole tent was lit up. Henry was groaning, and Indian Bob was bending over her with a cup of foul-smelling green tea. "Cactus tea," he said.

"She needs HalfLife™," I said.

"Cactus tea," he said again, as if it were the Indian verion of the same thing. And it seemed to work. She groaned and straightened and went back to sleep.

I went outside, into the blasting sun and cold wind. The bug was still in my pocket. It felt so good I couldn't keep my hands off it. I looked around for a jug or a jar. But what was the point? Nothing seemed to do any good.

I stuck it to the side of the van and watched it slide down, underneath, looking for a place to hide. I would have to deal with it later. But first—we had a funeral to attend to.

Indian Bob had already opened the van and started up the hill, with our Bob in his arms. I followed, pulling Homer in the Radio Flyer™. It was a bright, clear, sunshiny day. Behind me, the teepee snapped and flapped like a sail. We stopped at the gate and I put the shovels into the wagon with

Homer. "Something smells interesting," she said.

I decided to bring the whiskey along and wedged it into the wagon. "One problem," I said, as I followed Bob into the cemetery, under the bright HAPPY HUNTING GROUND sign. "We need our Bob to start the van."

"I can start it for you."

"But you're not going with us."

"Then just don't shut it off," Bob said. He set our Bob down between two open graves and pulled a shovel out of the wagon. "Pick your spot."

"Shouldn't you?"

"Whatever. This one, then." We settled on one, and while Bob unrolled Bob from the rug, I scratched the death date— October 15 (I was guessing here; I hadn't kept track of the days since we had left New York) 20—, into the cross with a cotter pin pulled from the wagon tongue. Then we laid Bob as straight as possible in the grave.

It was a little short, but he was a little bent.

Indian Bob bowed his head, and I did the same. He said something in a language I didn't understand, and passed me the HeyGoodLookin'.

"Something smells cold," said Homer. She was becoming a regular preacher. We covered Bob up and finished the whiskey and started down the hill.

Indian Bob went first. He heard the screaming first; he started to run. By the time I got to the teepee he was standing in the doorway, blocking the door.

"Don't come in," he said. "Let me handle this. I know what to do. You'll just be in the way."

"Way of what!?"

"Bob's girl. She's having a baby."

Chapter 34

A year went by.
        Then another.
        Most of the participants in the Round Table thought that Mr. Bill had lost all interest in the project; that the disputes and disagreements of the final days had sunk the project altogether, leaving them with only their memories and, of course, their million. The news about Damaris ended (by law) when she was formally spot-welded into her special cell and put on HalfLife™, on April 20, 20—. The welding was done by a member of The Loved Ones, Inc., under the Victims Rights Amendment to the Constitution. The procedure was "supervised" by a certified union welder (AFL/CIO) and corrections officer, even though the member of The Loved Ones, Inc., (chosen by lot) was an experienced jackleg welder who traveled with a Japanese soft wheat harvesting team as an in-field combine mechanic. Little was heard of Mr. Bill. Always eccentric, he grew even more reclusive.

The Alexandrians stayed in the news, however. Bombings, sloshing, slashing, and burnings were a weekly event, especially in Europe, where American films and "immigrant" art especially were targeted along with the works of the Old (and new) Masters. The Alexandrians in the Far East took on an anti-American and anti-European cast as well. Tokyo's Hideki Museum, with its collection of Fauvist and Cubist art, was burned to the ground. Security was tightened at every museum; attendance dropped steeply. Attacks on concert halls created panic in Indonesia. A Michael Jackson concert was stormed by an "Alexandrian" mob and the aged entertainer barely escaped with his life. In Shanghai and Seattle, thugs roamed the multiplexes, paid bounties by rival film companies. There were rumors of killer viruses on rap CDs. France's Disneyland was attacked by missiles, killing over a hundred people, four of them children. All this was done in the name of the Alexandrians.

At the same time, new productions in the arts were up, not down. Revenues were up. Just as war invigorates industry, the worldwide war on the arts and entertainment was increasing revenues, production, and, it was claimed by some (and of course denied by others), creativity. War was a good thing, if it could be regulated, according to the Wall Street Journal, which called for a managed "Cold War on the Arts" which would put the "anarchistic and nativist" Alexandrians out of business before they did irreparable damage. The same cry, with different imagery, was taken up by Variety, which called for an internationally monitored "Slash and Burn" program that could lead to renewal and, most important, "sustainability" in the arts and entertainment.

Chapter 35

I took Homer for a walk, all the way down to the interstate (such as it was, drifted with sand and blowing tumbleweeds) and back up the hill. The screaming got worse, so we did it again. Finally it was quiet inside the teepee. We waited in the lot by the van, not wanting to go in. "Something smells sweet," Homer said.

Indian Bob came to the doorway, carrying a bundle wrapped in a towel. It looked like a smaller version of Bob in his rug.

"She's sleeping," he said. He handed me the bundle. "Can you take him for a minute?"

The bundle was stiff. The face was covered up. "The baby is dead?"

"No no no," Bob said. "Just covered with blood. You could clean him up. There's a stock tank behind the cemetery. Go left at the gate."

"Something smells sweet," Homer said again.

"You wait here," I said to her. I started up toward the cemetery, carrying the stiff little bundle in my arms. I was afraid to look at it. Wasn't it supposed to be crying?

I turned left at the gate and walked around the outside of the cemetery. The stock tank was behind the hill, under a windmill that turned slowly with a rattling sound, even though there didn't seem to be any wind.

I unrolled the towel. The baby wasn't exactly a baby. It was a little man, about the size of an Oscar™ or a large sneaker, a twelve or thirteen. He was bald all over and wrinkled, like a fingertip that's been in the

THE PICKUP ARTIST   181

bathtub too long. His eyes were closed. His penis was almost
an inch long. His legs were skinny and he was covered with
blood.

He was light as a feather. I could hold him in one hand. I
dipped him in the water and he opened his eyes and said,
"Yup!"

I dipped him again, and wipe the blood off his legs, his
bottom, even his little penis, which got alarmingly hard.
Most babies are fat but this one was skinny. Most babies are
cute but this one was ugly. I wet a corner of the towel and
washed his tiny face. Something was watching me—

I turned and saw two antelopes, standing under the windmill. I shook the towel at them and they turned tail and ran.

It was a bright, cold fall morning, probably approaching
the end of October. I felt oddly peaceful, even though I had
only until the end of the month to find the album and return
it. I was confident that I could think of a story to explain my
absence, the shootings, the misdemeanor club. Meanwhile,
Homer seemed to be improving, not dying, and I had gotten
my trip to the West. Look how the rocky world glistened in
the sun! The water in the stock tank! The antelopes! They
had stopped a few feet away and were studying me again.

Here I am, I thought. "Here I am."

"M'lenny," said the little man. I couldn't call him a baby,
even in my thoughts. I dried him off and wrapped him in the
towel and started back around the hill toward the teepee. At
the cemetery gate, I met Indian Bob.

"I thought we heard you yelling," Bob said.

"Not me." Then I heard the yelling, and all my good feelings were gone, scattered like dry leaves before a wind. It was
coming from the cemetery. It was our Bob.

"No, no!" He was sitting up in his grave, with dust and
sand in his hair and eyes and face. His bony hands were
locked together and he was waving them in circles in front of
his face.

"Oh no!" he said. "No!"

"I told you that stuff was addictive," said Indian Bob.

"We need to cover him back up," I said. I set the little man down by the gate, still wrapped in his towel, and grabbed a shovel. "Come on!"

Indian Bob got the other shovel. Bob didn't seem to be in any danger of climbing out of his grave. He was just sitting there, saying "no, no, no," over and over. His eyes were wide open, not closed like they were when he had been sprayed with LastRites™. That gave me some hope that we could get him buried before Henry heard the commotion.

His eyes were like raisins. As a matter of fact, a crow sitting on a plastic cross nearby was eyeing them hungrily.

I tried pushing him down in the grave, but his knees came up, throwing more dirt out of the hole.

"What if we turn him on his side?" Bob suggested. I enlarged the hole, and we pushed him down, with his butt sticking out into the V.

"No!" he said. "No! Not this!"

"Dirt!" I said. Indian Bob starting shoveling it in and kicking it in at the same time.

"Wait."

We both stopped and straightened up and turned around. It was Henry. She was holding the little man in one arm and he was tugging at her bluebird sweater (which was covered with vague blue shapes) trying to get under it.

She reached under it herself and pulled out the sprayette of LastRites™. "Let's see what he wants," she said.

"No way!" I said. I grabbed for it and she tucked it back into her bra. "We know what he wants. He's dead. He wants to be alive."

"I tell you, that stuff's addictive," said Bob. "It lodges in the tissues, like dioxin."

Henry was kneeling by the grave. She set the little man down on the dirt and he clutched at her sweater to keep from falling in. "We don't need the stuff anyway," she said. "Bob, can you hear me?"

He closed his eyes. "I'm dead, that's it, isn't it!?"

"You told me you were taking care of me for Panama," she said. "You said you were an Alexandrian."

"I'm sorry," said Bob. "I wanted you for my own."

"So where is Panama? You don't even know, do you?"

"I'm sorry!" He was shaking his head, flinging dry dirt out of his mouth. "Don't bury me! Being dead is bad enough!"

"Yup!" said the little man.

"They brought you home," said Indian Bob. "This is the Indian Bob Cemetery. This is where you belong."

"No!"

"This is where he belongs," I said, picking up my shovel.

"I've got an idea," said Indian Bob. He walked toward the gate and beckoned for us to follow. "Can he hear us?"

"Who knows!" said Henry.

"Cremation," said Indian Bob. "There are a million crematoriums in Vegas. You can mail the ashes back to me."

"Vegas?" said Henry. "Is that where the Alexandrians are?"

"I don't know," said Bob. "I was just guessing." But I could tell he was lying. I wasn't surprised. I had suspected Vegas all along.

Twenty minutes later we were loading our stuff into the van. Bob was wrapped in the rug again. The little man was dressed in a towel, like a toga, still tugging at Henry's sweater, which now had several vague little wingless bluebirds flying across it like missiles.

She seemed happier now that her baby was born. Though she didn't seem to like the baby—the little man.

"Will somebody get him off me!" she said. He was standing on her arm, trying to reach down the neck of the sweater.

"He's hungry," I said.

"Well, I am not a cow!"

"I've got an idea," said Indian Bob. He seemed full of

ideas. He went into the teepee and came back out with a twenty-four-ounce can of chocolate flavored Mighty Pudding™. "One of the Bobs was into this stuff, it's a health food. He wanted it buried with him."

"And?" I said, accusingly.

"It seemed like a waste. Maybe the baby will eat it." He gave the cans to Henry, who opened one while I helped slide Bob, wrapped in the rug, into the van.

"Something smells good," said Homer. Henry opened another can for her.

Soon we were ready to go. Indian Bob gave me three chips, two whites and a red, to cover the cremation and the postage. Then he pressed the starter for us so we wouldn't have to unroll our Bob.

But the van wouldn't start.

It was dead.

"Maybe Henry should spray it with LastRites™," I said. It was a joke. Everybody got it (except for Homer and the little man, of course, and our Bob) but nobody laughed. Henry's bluebirds were fading when Indian Bob stepped in: "I have an idea."

It was a can of gas-o-line. "This will get you to a station," he said as he poured it into a little opening at the rear of the van. Whoa! I had never actually smelled anything like it before. Or had I? It was new and yet somehow familiar, a smell so strong you could actually see it in the air. The engine started with a grinding, then a popping, and then a whirring sound. "We use gas-o-line all the time here off the grid. Head south"—he pointed—"and you'll eventually hit another interstate."

"Thanks for everything," I said as we started down the hill.

"Yup," said the little man.

"Get off me!" said Henry.

"Something smells wonderful," said Homer. She meant the gas-o-line, which has an expansive smell like doors open-

ing, like a light coming on; like memory. I could still smell it
on my fingers.

Vegas. No longer the wealthiest city in the hemisphere,
but still the most historical, it beckoned us from across
the horizon as it had beckoned all along. We still didn't
know it for sure yet, though. We had a few more roads to
find.

"I told you that stuff was addictive," I told Henry, as we
pulled onto the empty interstate heading south and west.
More than empty—the road was rough, humped with drifted
sand. Now that we were off the grid the van's gas-o-line
engine made a *pop-pop-popp*ing sound that reminded me
of . . . what? Then of course I remembered: the bug, stuck
somewhere underneath. From its adversary I had become its
accomplice.

Our top speed was about sixty kph. The gas-o-line engine
in lectros is supposedly an auxiliary, designed to charge the
flywheel. But I didn't know the proper way to use it. Should I
pull over and let it charge, or should I keep limping along in
the hope of finding a station?

I kept limping.

Homer lay in her Radio Flyer™ in the back, looking at me
in the mirror with her big, brown eyes.

Bob was quiet at last. He looked like a tube worm rolled
up in his rug.

Henry sat staring straight ahead. The little man sat on her
lap eating Mighty Pudding™ with his tiny fingers and occasionally plucking at the front of the bluebird sweater. The
bluebird count was back down to one, and that one was fading. "He didn't even know where Panama was," she said
gloomily.

"You want to drive?" I asked. "I'll hold him."

Off the grid, we had to pull over to switch. The little man
stood on my lap, holding onto the front of my shirt, staring

out the side window. I must have slept. When I woke up we were slowed to forty kph. The road was straight. Where before there had been sand showing through the grass, there was now grass showing through the sand. The sun was so bright, the whole sky seemed to give off light, like unpainted metal. The highway shimmered in the heat.

"Something smells shitty," said Homer. I smelled it, too. My knee was wet. I held the little man at arm's length and a couple of tiny turds rolled out of the towel.

"Yup," he said.

"He's disgusting," said Henry.

"He's your son," I said.

"He's Panama's son, you mean."

"Yup," said the little man.

TAKE THIS ENTRANCE TO INTERSTATE 77 WEST," said the Finder.

It was noon and we had finally reached the east-west connection. "That proves that we're on the way to Vegas," I said. If the Finder had sent us east I would have worried.

Henry was too busy driving to answer. We were off the north-south interstate but still not on the east-west. The problem was, there was no entrance ramp. Trucks whizzed by, perfectly spaced. Our little van rocked in their draft.

Henry steered the van off the road, onto the desert. "Where are you going?" I asked. I didn't like being off the grid, much less off the road.

"West," she said. "The Finder says west, so we go west."

The desert made a better road than the interstate had made. We cruised at thirty to forty kph, following the fence line of the interstate. There were a few rough spots. Once the little man fell off my lap, but he quickly got up again. He liked to stand on my knees, hold onto the dash, and stare out the windshield. Once we found a hole in the fence and tried to get onto the pavement, but the shoulder was shielded. As soon as the van nosed out over the concrete there was a zapping sound from underneath.

"Something smells bad," said Homer.

Smoke! Henry backed up, fast. I thought of the bug, hiding under there.

The trucks roared by, one by one, electronically chained in hundred meter multiples, rocking the van but throwing up less dust than we threw up. I could tell by the grim look on Henry's face, and the fading of her last bluebird, that she was getting hungry. So was I. Plus I wondered how long we could go without either gas-o-line or grid current.

It was late afternoon before I saw a faraway figure on a long stalk. "A flying horse!"

"No, it's a dinosaur," said Henry. "No, a clam."

"Whatever," I said. "It means gas-o-line."

The station was on a raised platform, accessible by the interstate, but Henry was able to pull up from the desert by shifting into careful. We pulled in between two concrete islands just as the attendant was locking himself into a little booth.

I got out and knocked on the glass. The attendant shook his head. I showed him my last ten. He nodded and I shoved it, folded, through a slot in the door.

With a hose I filled the van with gas-o-line until the attendant knocked on the glass and told me to stop. There was that smell again. Every time was like the first time; you never got used to it. After the hose was hung up, I looked underneath for the bug. Gone: scorched and lost, probably when the van hit the shield. I felt surprisingly sad. I missed the little red eye.

Henry came out of the Gift Shoppe which the attendant had neglected to lock. She had a smile on her face and several bluebirds were visible again; one was even flapping its wings in a slow, distracted sort of way. She was carrying the little man on her left forearm, like a falcon in an old movie. He was dressed—in tiny cowboy hat and chaps and a fringed shirt. He was barefoot, though; and still tugging at her sweater.

"I found a cowboy doll," she said. "Stop it!"

"Yup," said the little man.

"What about the boots?"

"They were solid wood. No inside."

"He needs a diaper."

"He learns fast. He's already off the Mighty Pudding™."

"He has teeth?"

"I'm going to have to think of a name for him pretty soon."

It was my turn to drive. The entrance wasn't shielded, and I was able to move onto the interstate, and switch off the gas-o-line. Now that we had plenty, we didn't need it. Much of life is that way, it often seems.

I slotted into the fast lane and let the van drive itself. "Something smells nice," said Homer, who was awake. It could have been Bob, who had taken on a whole new character after his brief sojourn in the grave. Instead of bad meat he now smelled like fresh dirt, desert, stone and sage, wind and sand, sort of like men's cologne.

I drove until dark and the lights came on and I kept on driving, buoyed by snores from the back and the front alike. Only the little man and I were awake. There were no lights, no mohotels, no no-queries, no flee markets, no nothing but rock and sand and mountains like bone or cloud, always far away.

I heard a *pop-pop-pop*, at the back of the van. I was surprised at the sudden warmth I felt, which was almost like the tingle in my hand when I picked up the bug. The bug was back, hiding under the van, and I was secretly, mysteriously, surprisingly glad. Did I *want* to be followed?

Don't we, secretly, mysteriously, surprisingly, all?

I must have fallen asleep and dreamed because when I woke up, I had an erection. The van was humming along at a steady hundred and ten. I was still in the driver's seat. Henry had finally shut up and gone to sleep. There was a glow in the distance, under the horizon, ahead. I thought it was dawn until I remembered we were heading west. A forest fire? But there were no trees. A skirmish? A pile-up of trucks? A volcanic event? Then the little man, who was standing on Henry's lap, spoke his first new word (after "yup") and solved the mystery, such as it was.

"Vegas," he said in a voice that was at once deep and small.

Chapter 36

*T*he United Nations International High Commission on Arts and Entertainment was established by a vote of the General Assembly on March 12, 20—. Its mandate was to devise a plan acceptable to all that would "prune the arts in a fair and nonviolent fashion." Though the High Commission (or HC as it was called in the fanciful and self-congratulatory account written by its first chairperson) was accountable to no organization, person, or government, it held "extended and strictly confidential consultations" with representatives of NATO, NAFTA, the Pacific Rim Consortium, the US government, Microsofts One and Two, Disney, Universal Studios, and "others that must and will remain unnamed." It is certain, though of course never confirmed, that the "others unnamed" included members of the Round Table. The HC seemed to have little immediate effect on the level of violence, and in fact the Alexandrian attacks intensified, particularly in California, where three libraries were burned in one week, and the archives of the Dr. Seuss Foundation were stolen and dumped into the sea. A seascape artist in Key West was arrested for attacking his own gallery with a gas-o-line bomb. No major company was insuring paintings anymore.

The High Commission, which was, like the UN that gave it birth, advisory only, advised the establishment of an international agency with "appropriate police powers," that would delete "an unnamed number" of art works yearly. This recommendation met with such hostility from the music, publishing, and film industries (Camilla Brown of Sony called it "the death penalty for art," a cry that was ironically later used in its favor) that it was quickly downgraded to a "recommendation for further study," which was well within the mandate of the High Commission. The US President was asked to chair and finance the study, since the US was "the source" of the steady stream of arts and entertainment that was inundating the world, and any enforcement or reduction would have to be within the US legal framework. This recommendation was not at the time seen as the compliment that it was. The Academy of Motion Picture Arts and Sciences issued a statement claiming that the problem was a "worldwide culture of violence" rather than information overload. Congress reacted with predictable mindless hostility, blocking President Weed's nomination of former film star Apparent Phoenix to the HC's investigatory commission with an electronic filibuster. The stalemate threatened the prestige, the funding and even the existence of the High Commission. Then an act of extraordinary and graphic cruelty, the grisly assassination of the world's most prolific novelist, Gus Pope, in 20—, broke the stalemate and opened the door to long-needed change.

Chapter 37

Vegas. We saw the glow before we saw the lights, and we saw the lights before we saw the buildings, and we saw the buildings, shimmering like a mirage, dancing in the sunstretched and sunbleached air, long before we saw the sandy tangle of streets and lots and plots and real estate—the first to successfully secede from the U.S.—out of which they rose with all the grandeur and mystery pure pleasure could summon.

"Vegas was once the second richest city in America, and for a brief period of about two years, the second largest," Henry said. "It was third in the consumption of electricity and fourth in water. It was second in immigration and fifth in emigration."

"Amazing," I said. Little of this was new to me, but Henry seemed to feel the need to talk.

It was dawn. She sat beside me with the little man standing on the seat between her knees, staring straight ahead as we sped west across sand and salt, dust and rock and stone, as if fleeing the rising sun. She was friendlier, now that she had a child. I no longer had to do most of the talking; though must of Henry's conversation was dry and librarianlike.

"All that was when it was in the U.S.," she went on. "It was the first city-state to secede from the Union, and four years later the first (six months before Venice!) to be admitted to the United Nations as a world city with its own passport, customs, currency, and fees."

And off the grid, of course: our first problem was getting in. "TAKE EAST GATE EXIT," said the Finder. The

exit put us on a long boulevard cut like an arrow, or a scar,
through a tangle of mostly abandoned walled suburbs, some
of them still patrolled by Burns™, the amoebalike security
molds that were once painted like warning signs on every
Level Two apartment complex in America, until it was discovered that they became water soluble after a year in the
sun.

"GET IN LINE AT EAST GATE," said the Finder. "WELCOME TO
VEGAS. THIS ENDS SEARCH UNIT TWENTY. PRESS ESCAPE TO EXIT
GEO SEARCH. PRESS MENU FOR A NEW SEARCH."

There was no line at East Gate. According to Henry, who
was a veritable fount of information, "Most of Vegas's visitors enter from the south and west." She went on to explain
why. Meanwhile, the van was waved to a stop by a woman
in a Vegas-style customs jumpsuit with a clipboard and name
tag: Karen the Inquisitive.

"How long you entering for?"

I made a quick guess: "A week."

"That'll be fifteen hundred."

My pained expression wasn't faked. "Can't it just go on
the EzGo?"

"You get it back in chips, tokens, coupons," she said. "As
soon as you check into the hotel. What hotel are you staying
at?"

"We haven't decided," I said. "We already have chips." I
showed her the two whites and the red the last Indian Bob
had given me for the cremation.

That was a mistake. "Indian stuff," she said, shaking her
head. "Discounted like crazy. What's that smell?"

"Something smells peculiar," said Homer from the back of
the van.

Karen the Inquisitive stuck her head in the window. "Is
that a talking dog?"

"Karen the Inquisitive," said Henry, reading her name tag.
"Every citizen in Vegas wears a name tag. The descriptive
honorific is optional."

"Is that a dead body?"

"We're here for the crematoriums," Henry said. "Vegas has more crematoriums per capita than any other world city."

"Why didn't you say so? I can give you a one-day, then," Karen said, peeling a decal off her clipboard and sticking it onto our windshield. "But remember, you can't bring the body out!"

"We'll remember," I said. I was about to drive off when she held up her hand. I heard a beep from under the van, and I looked out and down. We were being scanned. A tech in a customs jumpsuit was poking under the van with a long rod.

"Got it!" he said. He pulled it out the rod, and there, stuck on the end, its little wings beating furiously and its little red eye flashing in panic—was the bug.

I cringed as it was dropped into a stoneware pot. I cringed as the lid slammed shut, and was sealed with a steel band. I cringed again to see the pot placed in a long metal drawer with several other pots, and then the drawer itself slid into a slot in the concrete wall.

The gate lurched up and Karen the Inquisitive waved us on.

"Good riddance," said Henry.

"Vegas," said the little man, from his station standing on Henry's knee.

"Something smells wonderful," said Homer.

"It's gas-o-line," I said, as we merged into the circular, counterclockwise traffic. We were still on lectric, but most of the cars and buses and taxis were belching invisible (and not so invisible) smoke and fumes.

Our sticker was only good for a day. I wasn't even sure what I was looking for. My album? Panama? The Finder was no help. We were on our own.

We drove twice around the Loop to get the feel of the place. First there were the big casino hotels: the Palladium, the Coaster, the Millennium, the Rialto, the Pentium, the

THE PICKUP ARTIST   195

Fantasia, the Imperial, and so on, and so forth—each one taller and gaudier than the others.

The little man, in particular, seemed fascinated. "M'Lenny," he said, craning his little head to look up; or at least that's what it sounded like he said.

"Lenny?" said Henry, making a face as if the syllables tasted bad. "Is that his name, then?"

"M'Lenny."

And Lenny it was, from then on in. Next (noon on the clock of the Loop) came the commercial strip—the United Nations; the Taj Too; the Palace of Diana, entered through the outstretched, caring Hand; the Vatican, with the spiralling lines watched over by Swiss Guards with their light sabers; the Louvre. After that (nine on the clock) came the theme parks and family attractions, various and new: Circus Max; Mister Rogers; Heaven's Gate with its giant rotating Nike shoes; Flirts; Chez Spelling; Hooters Unltd (visible for miles). The bottom (six o'clock) of the Loop was a one- and two-story smudge of marriage and divorce chalets, new and used car parlors, budget mohotels, and assorted gift shops and quickie crematoriums.

I pulled in at the first crematorium I saw, under a "flaming" neon sign.

"Something smells burned," said Homer.

Henry woke up all of a sudden and saw the sign: KWIK KREME. "What's the hurry?" she asked.

"Let's get this part over with," I said. "It makes us legit."

"We won't be able to get the van started again."

"I'll leave it running."

The proprietor inside at the long desk was named Womack the Empathetic, according to his name tag. He accompanied me back out to the van. "Does the rug come with him?" he asked.

"No way," said Henry.

"It qualifies you for a discount."

"How much?" I asked.

"Ten percent. The rug looks useable. Plus, we get the shoes, the fillings, whatever's in the pockets, the prosthetics, the trace minerals, etcetera, and you get the savings."

"Savings from what?" I asked. "I mean, what is the actual price?"

"The price will surprise you. Surprise and please. Is he family?"

"Sort of," said Henry. "I mean, he is; we're not. Exactly."

"You can't go strictly by price when family is concerned," said Womack the Empathetic. "The important thing is to listen to your feelings."

"Something smells burned," said Homer, again.

The price, when we finally got to it, was exactly everything we had: two whites and a red. And that was with the discount for the rug. "This Indian stuff is worthless," Womack explained. "They should never have sold out to the Danes."

"What about the ashes?" I asked as Womack and I carried him into the lobby, rolled up in the rug. "Do you give us something to put them in?"

"Better than that," said Womack. He showed me a plastic urn with a UPC code imprinted between the two handles. "Second Day Air is included, for those who are in a hurry to send their loved one on home," he said. "Engraved, too. What's the name?"

"That would be up to her," I said, glancing at Henry. "Robert or Bob?"

"Bob," Henry said. "Our Bob. My Bob."

Something smells sticky," said Homer.

Womack was pulling a blackened mesh drawer out of the wall. It was like the drawer into which the bug had been put away. Little crisp pieces of stuff were stuck to the mesh here and there.

I helped Womack the Empathetic unroll Bob from the rug and lay him in the drawer. His arm cracked when we pulled it down to his side. Womack was just about to push the drawer in when his assistant—Carla the Energetic—came into the lobby and started spraying the flowers with an aerosol can.

It must have been the hiss of the spray. Bob sat up. His mouth fell open and his raisinlike eyes closed, then opened again. "Oh no!" he said.

Carla the Energetic dropped the can and fled.

"It's okay!" said Henry. "We're here."

"Okay?! Since when is dead *okay*?! Where am I?"

"Vegas," I said.

"You're going to *cremate* me? Just because I lied to you?!"

"It's because you're dead," Henry said. "You didn't want to be buried, remember?"

"But burned? Incinerated? I can't stand it! This is going from bad to worse."

"It's death," I said. "No happy endings here."

"Easy for you to say!" said Bob. "You're not about to be fucking burned like fucking Joan of . . ."

"Tell him to watch his language," said Womack the Empathetic. "And listen, there's no way I can cremate him if he's complaining. Have you been using LastRites™? It's addictive. Plus it has a residual effect in the lungs."

"I know," I said.

"I'm dead! I'll be dead from now on. Forever!"

"It's just the deal," said Henry. "It's okay."

"It's *not* okay!" Though his dessicated body had ceased, or almost ceased, to smell, Bob's breath was fouler than ever. I had to keep backing up just to talk to him.

"He has to be completely dead," said Womack, who was standing in the doorway, shaking his head. "There are regulations, even here in Vegas."

"He really is pretty much dead," said Henry. "This is just a residual effect of the LastRites™ which saturates the alveolar tissues."

But there was no convincing Womack, who helped me carry Bob back to the van.

We got our chips back, minus one white which Womack claimed as a restocking fee. We kept the urn, which was already engraved "Our Bob."

"Restocking what!?" said Henry. "What a rip-off!"

The sunlight was brutal, but we had left the van running—otherwise how could Homer and Lenny have survived? It was the middle of the afternoon and we were, I realized, starved. Luckily there was a McDonald's a few blocks down from the Kwik Kreme.

I shut the van off this time, since we still had Bob to restart it. I left the climate control on, though.

The white chip bought us two cones of bush meat, one of which I split with Homer. Henry split the other one with the little man, Lenny, who was off the Mighty Pudding™ entirely. He was still pulling at her sweater; she was still batting him away; but they were both less energetic about it.

We sat in McDonald's and watched the traffic glide by. We were the only customers.

"Maybe we should just dump him in a lot somewhere and send the urn with some ashes to Indian Bob," I said.

Henry shook her head. "He was my friend."

"Even though he lied? Even though he used you?"

"He loved me. That's why he lied to me."

We drove around the Loop three times before finding Panama. On our second circuit, as our lowlite was already beginning to glow, dim red, like the ashes of a finished fire, my heart gave an unexpected little lurch when I heard an unexpected (but not entirely!) *pop-pop-pop*!

"Your pal," Henry said.

The bug was back. I felt a familiar, expectant tingling in my hands and the backs of my knees. I kept my eyes on the road instead of the rearview, but still, I could imagine it, sliding down toward the warm undercarriage (modulating its magnetism to allow it to slide downward over metal surfaces). Red eye glowing.

"Something smells pretty," said Homer, her big brown eyes on mine in the rearview. Homer understood!

We drove by Kwik Kreme again, but without, of course, stopping. We started our third circuit. The traffic was picking up and it was getting dark, which meant Vegas was coming to life. Everything here was backward. Even the highway ran counterclockwise. It was getting dark as we approached the Strip (three o'clock) and the grand hotels were just lighting up in a spectacular show—Palladium, Coaster, Rialto, Pentium, Fantasia, Imperial, Astro, Belair, Delight, Ensign . . . all aglitter except for two, which were (according to the Vegas Guide, which I only read much later) scheduled for the periodic demolitions that made way for new attractions. The Millennium and the Flamingo stood out like bad teeth.

"M'Lenny," said Lenny as the stream of traffic slowed, piched between the soaring towers.

"How come he only learns one word at a time?" Henry asked sourly. She never addressed Lenny directly.

"M'Lenny," he said again, jabbing at the windshield with one tiny finger.

"Something smells lucky," said Homer.

"That's it!" I said.

"What?" said Henry.

"The Millenium," I said, slotting toward the exit lane.

Lenny nodded. "M'Lenny'm." He looked up at Henry and grabbed at her breasts; she slapped him away.

I pulled up by a low concrete wall between two abandoned lectros. To my mind, they made us less conspicuous. I shut off the van.

Instead of looking happy, Henry looked scared.

The Millennium was a black glass tower, twenty-four stories high. The signs and displays and windows all were dark.

The only light came from the last rays of the setting sun reflecting off the top floors.

"Wait here," I said. I got out and walked toward the door. Halfway across the lot, I looked back. Lenny was following me. When had he learned to walk?

He was wobbling, trying to run.

I scooped him up and continued toward the entrance. It was a revolving door, sealed with EternityTape™. Nothing but darkness inside. I could barely make out a few dead palms and a turned-off waterfall.

A rat ran across the floor.

This could be, I thought, *the perfect hide-out.* I put my eye to the glass and I heard the hum of air conditioners and, far off, what sounded like bells. I stuck my hand in the revolving door's rubber seal, which gave just enough to admit my fingertips, and felt cool, moist air.

Lenny was pulling at my shirt. I set him down.

"Yup," he said—the first of his three words. Then "Vegas," then "Millenium." Then he handed me his cowboy hat and before I could stop him—though I had no intention of stopping him, and would not have if I could—slipped by the seal, into the inner wedge of the revolving door. Then he slipped by the next seal and was lost in the darkness.

I put my fingers against the glass and watched until I saw something—it could have been the rat, or could have been Lenny—scurry across the inner lobby floor. Then all was darkness, silence, stillness. I waited for what seemed hours and then went back to the van. Luckily, Henry was asleep, so I had no explanations to make.

Not that she would have missed him.

Sleep is the nibbling surf of Death, the darkness that deletes us one day, one night at a time. The Sea of Nothingness into which, streaming dreams like bubbles, we sink. I was dreaming, and in my dream Henry had taken off her bluebird bra to reveal a smaller bra under it, covered with bright-winged ruby-eyed . . .

Pop-pop-pop.

The bug! My hand was tingling and when I reached into my pocket, there it was, the bug. How had it escaped from Customs? How had it gotten into the van?

Pop-pop-pop.

But I was dreaming again.

I opened my eyes and saw the first gleams of dawn on Reagan Peak to the north.

The pop was actually a tap.

Tap-tap-tap.

It was the little man, Lenny, tapping on the window of the car.

He was no longer dressed as a cowboy but wearing a small suit complete with necktie. He also, I noticed right away, had shoes.

The van had rotary hand cranks. I rolled the window down.

"Panama," he said. "Vegas Millennium Panama yup!"

Chapter 38

The gruesome, indeed, monstrous manner of Pope's death, not to mention the bizarre circumstances of its discovery, outraged even the captured Alexandrians, legitimized all those who were looking for a remedy (no matter what their motives), and silenced all opposition, at least temporarily. The House minority leader broke ranks with her own filibuster, holding up a print-out of Time *ezine's infamous (and almost-censored) cover illustrating Pope's gruesome reassembled remains, and called for "speedy and decisive" congressional action. The opposition folded, at least for the moment. Apparent Phoenix was confirmed for the High Commission's study subgroup, and simultaneously made secretary of the newly-created cabinet-level Department of Arts and Entertainment. The department was "advisory only" also, and it has often been speculated that this ceremonial appointment was the extent of the president's wishes; that no one wished to change* anything, *least of all her. Events, however, were running ahead of wishes, and certainly ahead of US politics.*

The Deletion Engine was unveiled at a press conference in the grand lobby of the Virgin Atlantic Hotel in New York City. It was about the size of a car, although it had no wheels and was brought out on a maglev skid. The four windows (two large, two small) were for looking in, not out. It was the product of an Austin software consulting group that had been working for twelve years on the project, predating (for those who knew) the Round Table and even the Alexandrians themselves. They had originally been hired by the

US Department of Corrections to devise a random lottery generator that would correct for race and class and choose the victims by lot from the pool of those sentenced to die. The Deletion Engine had unfortunately been rendered irrelevant before it was perfected, when the mandatory death penalty was introduced and the DOC was privatized. The Austin group stayed together, however, under new management, adapting their machine to solve yet another public crisis, thanks to the public-spirited efforts of their employer . . . And here the chief engineer introduced the owner of the Virgin Atlantic Hotel (and indeed of the entire chain, which had spun off from the airline after the unfortunate and unprecedented mid-air collision, the first involving two planes of one carrier), the reclusive billionaire known as Mr. Bill. In the tradition of Rockefeller, Vanderbilt, and Carnegie (as he explained), Mr. Bill had always wanted to use his billions to promote the general welfare, particularly in connection with the two great causes closest to his heart, Corrections and art. The Deletion Engine was conceived in one and born in the other, said Mr. Bill, who seemed as puzzled as anyone in the press as to how the Deletion Engine actually worked. He was pleased, however, to offer it to the American people as an instrument that might be of some use to the new department in its efforts to liberate the nation from the effects of information overload and the violence it had caused and was continuing to cause. And so forth, etcetera. No questions from the press were entertained. Instead, Mr. Bill produced Apparent Phoenix himself, who was "pleased to receive, on behalf of his department, this ingenious device which," and so forth, etcetera. By the time Mr. Pheonix had expressed his thanks the press was gone, leaving only their photographers, who were busily taking pictures of the Engine as it was being crated for shipment by rail to Washington, DC.

Chapter 39

enry wanted to take her time. First it was lipstick, then eye shadow. Then she muttered, "You're in for a thrill," and pulled her bluebird sweater off over her head. Her bluebird bra was already familiar; I had seen it in a drawer. There was of course no need to tell her that.

It reminded me of my dream. I slipped my hand into my pocket, and felt a pleasant tingling. The bug! It had been no dream.

Using the last of the water from the last of the jugs the last of the Indian Bobs had given us, Henry washed her hair, and then her neck and shoulders and under her arms, while Lenny watched, entranced, and I pretended not to.

If before she had seemed terrified at the prospect of finally meeting Panama, now she seemed almost merry.

"Something smells sad," said Homer.

"Don't worry, you're going with us," I said, as I lifted her Radio Flyer™ out of the van. Then, while no one was watching, I palmed the bug out of my pocket and stuck it under the van. I didn't want to carry it in my pocket on this most, hopefully, momentous day. I loved the feeling it gave me, but it was distracting.

By the time our little entourage was ready, the sun was high over the Days Inn to the east and the Vegas air was heating up like oil in a lava lamp. Henry had pulled on her sweater and her breasts seemed bigger and shapelier than ever. Lenny thought so too: he was tugging at her bluebird sweater, and she was slapping him away—but distractedly.

Now instead of merry she seemed almost bored. The blue-birds were vague and gray.

We left Bob rolled up in his rug in the back of the van, with the climate control on to keep the smell down. I led the way with the Radio Flyer™ and Homer right behind me. Henry followed, with Lenny perched on her arm.

"Panama Press Lenny!" Lenny said into the intercom—a grille over a door to the left of the main revolving door, which was sealed forever with EternityTape™.

The door buzzed open and Lenny and Henry stepped inside. I was just about to follow when I heard a *pop-pop-pop*. It was the bug, already crawling to the underside of the Radio Flyer™. The door was about to close, so I rushed through.

Inside, it was dark. No, light. The floor was dark, but the darkness faded to light above. The interior was open, a vast space disappearing into a sort of soft haze that hid the upper balconies. A turned-off waterfall on the far wall lent the space an almost natural air.

The floor looked like a checkerboard: pale squares marked where the slot machines and blackjack and craps tables and roulette wheels had been. All gone.

To the left of the waterfall, a bullet-type elevator in a clear shaft hung from the upper floors like a glass vine.

It was coming down.

I could see a man inside. His arms were filled with books.

"Something smells crazy," said Homer. Lenny was silent and so was Henry.

We watched as the elevator came to a stop and opened, and a man stepped out: tall, thin, stooped, and bald on top, with a long ponytail of silver-gray hair. He squinted, as if everything he saw was a point size too small. He wore a gray jumpsuit and carried a stack of books, CDs, and videotapes in his arms.

"Panama?" I asked, looking toward Henry for confirmation. And it was clearly him, for she was already falling,

206   Terry Bisson

swooning, fainting, limb by limb—knees, hands, hips, into a
girl-shaped pile on the dusty floor. Lenny jumped free at the
last moment.

"Henrietta?" said Panama. He set down his books, tapes,
and CDs at the edge of the dry waterfall, then knelt to feel
her pulse, meanwhile gently swatting away Lenny, who was
trying to reach up under her bluebird sweater.

He looked from Henry to me.

"Are you Indian Bob?"

"Absolutely not. No way."

"Then you can help me get her upstairs." He picked up
Henry in his arms. "The boy can ride with the dog. Who are
you, then?"

"Shapiro. Hank Shapiro."

"Come on, then. You can bring the dog."

I pulled Homer and let Lenny ride.

The elevator sealed around us, a glass clamshell, and we
rose swiftly through the darkness, into the light. The half
light: for though it looked lighter above, it was dim when we
arrived.

Ding.

The elevator stopped on the nineteenth floor. The *ding*
woke Henry, and I wondered if she remembered the ominous, violent, indeed fatal *ding*s at her apartment building in
Brooklyn. But her eyes were filled with peace, not panic; and
it was not me she looked at but Panama.

She said nothing and closed her eyes again. Her bluebirds
were back, flying in formation, one on each breast, heading
west; or was it east?

Carrying her in his arms, Panama started down the open
tier toward the rooms, which were arranged around the central shaft. I followed, pausing to look over the rail. It was like
being in space, with infinity above and infinity below.
Though I had never been in space, I had sometimes imagined
it. Specks of dust floated through the air like planets, looking

THE PICKUP ARTIST   207

for a shaft of light in which to spin. It was as though the light itself had been darkened. I found out later it was polarized.

"This way."

I followed Panama and Henry into a small room with a double bed, a television, and a dresser. The bed was covered with books. Panama pointed imperiously with his chin, and I swept the books off the bed onto the floor.

"Something smells lovely," said Homer.

"Yup," said Lenny.

"Pull the covers down."

I did, and Panama laid her on the bed. She was smiling. He covered her up to her chin and turned to me. "You shouldn't have brought her here."

"You've got it backwards," I said. "It wasn't me who brought her here, but her who brought me here." I explained about the Williams and how I had followed it across the country. I left out where I had gotten it, but he figured that out by looking at my sky blue, one-stripe pants.

"A Bureau renegade. There's no place for you here, Shapiro."

"Fine," I said. "I have no interest in you or the other Alexandrians. All I want is the record, so I can return to New York and get my job back. I've still got a week until October rendering."

"That's wishful thinking," Panama said.

"What is?"

"All of it. Come, and I'll show you."

He led me to the next room on the tier. The bed and the dresser were stacked with books, CDs, a few oil paintings and prints, sheet music, old paperbacks, movies on video.

The next room was the same, or almost the same, with a garden sculpture (a saint with a bird) in one corner, and books and CDs spilling off the bed.

And the next.

And the next.

All the rooms were unlocked, and in every room there were books, CDs, sheet music, paintings, tapes, and even a few albums—piled on the bed, scattered on the floor, stacked in the bathroom, overflowing out of the closet.

Many in some, few in others, some in all. We stood at the railing, and Panama swept his hand out, then up, then down, as if he owned it all; and indeed, in his way, he did.

"The Millennium is a big place," he said. "Everything the Alexandrians have saved is here. For now." There were twenty-four floors, he told me, and twenty-four rooms on every floor. That made 576 rooms. A week wouldn't be enough time to go through them all.

But there was no reason I should have to. "Who brings all this stuff upstairs?" I asked.

"I do. I used to."

"Where is the latest stuff? My record arrived in the past few days. It would be recent."

"Recent has a different meaning here," Panama said. "This is Vegas. Off the clock. We get new stuff all the time, at least we used to, and I don't have time to log it in or sort it all."

"What about the other Alexandrians?"

"I'm the only one here."

"What about Henry? What about Bob?"

"Indian Bob? The one she knew?"

"Bob's outside," I said. "In our van. He's dead."

"Bob was never an Alexandrian," Panama said. "He was hardly even an Indian Bob. The Bobs are bootleggers. They bring one copy of everything the Bureau pulls—" He looked at the stripe on my pants. "—what *you* pickup artists pull, and they leave it on the loading dock. I sort it."

"In what order? Where does it go?"

"I'm a little behind," Panama said. "I'm too busy catching up to get ahead."

He smiled a thin smile, and I recognized a joke. A bureaucrat's joke. No wonder a librarian had fallen for him so hard.

"You mean my record could already be upstairs some-where?" I asked.

"Absolutely. Remember, there was one copy here already, before this recent bootleg you've been chasing. It could be in any one of these . . ." He suddenly looked alarmed, as if remembering something undone. "What did I do with the stuff I was carrying when you came in? Where did I put it?"

I was beginning to see that he was, to put it charitably, confused. But I was willing to help him, even though I could see that he wasn't going to be much help to me.

"In the lobby," I said.

In the elevator I noticed that there were buttons for twenty-five floors. "Forget the top one," Panama said. "It's not part of the hotel."

When we stepped out of the elevator into the lobby, I saw stacks of books and records, paintings and CDs in the shad-ows. There were several small piles of stuff in the basin of the turned-off waterfall. I couldn't tell which was the one he had last set down. They all looked different, but all the same.

"Which are the ones I set down?" Panama asked.

I pointed at one, at random. Panama scooped them up in one arm and headed for the elevator. Lenny ran after him.

And so I got to work. The great thing about records is that they have a unique size and shape, which meant that I didn't have to go through every item in every pile. I tried to keep track of the rooms, first by remembering the numbers, and then, when that began to seem excessive, by putting a soap mark on the dresser mirror. I used an X. Lucky for me, albums are rare. (Imagine if Williams had been an author, and my quarry a book!) It took me only minutes to toss a pile. Lucky for me, too, that there was plenty to eat, snacks anyway, in the rooms with their seemingly bottomless little minibars.

There was no day or night. I checked the loading dock

after every tier of rooms. It was a two-bay garage behind the lobby with a raised pier, on which Panama left little piles of books, records, CDs, and paintings that got removed, somehow. He seemed to be locked in a sort of circle. It was impossible to tell new from old, what I had tossed from what I hadn't. I never saw the Bobs bring anything in, and the big ferro-plastic door to the outside was always closed. I could see sunlight under it like an ingot of pure light.

I checked the lobby periodically. Mostly, though, I looked in the rooms, walking the tiers from two to twenty-four. Homer slept through it all, both eyes closed, her nose hanging over one end of the Radio Flyer™ and her tail over the other. Her head was still getting bigger; her body smaller. She ate less and less: mostly mixed nuts from the minibars. I slept whenever I felt myself circling that still, dark pool in which we dive to catch our dreams—clearing a bed, and sometimes finding a litle pile of books at my feet when I awoke! Had I missed Panama making his endless rounds?

I went by to see Henry a couple of times on nineteen, but she was always asleep, curled up under the covers, her bluebird sweater folded carefully on the pillow beside her. I barely thought of Bob, wrapped in the rug in the van. I barely thought of New York, or my job. Ex job? There are no clocks in the Millennium's rooms, and no windows, so I had no idea when it was day or when it was night. The inside of a Vegas casino, even a decommissioned one, induces a deep and dreamlike state, as I was to discover when I was awakened by an unfamiliar but familiar, terrifying sound.

Gunshots.

Tak-tak-tak.

The shots were followed by a cry: "Yup! Yup!"

There was another burst of fire—and then, silence.

Chapter 40

*P*eople in general, and the American people in particular, love three things: fairness, gambling, and machines; and by combining all three in one attractive package, the Deletion Engine made the acceptance of the Department of Arts and Entertainment much easier. It was later revealed that the order of events—the press conference, the presentation, the acceptance—had been orchestrated by Golden Boy, the same public relations firm that had been hired by the Victims' Rights Coalition in 20— to lobby successfully for the referendum that had made the death penalty mandatory in all cases where there was a loss of life or property worth more than a thousand (later amended to 1500). A department with a machine is a department with a mission, and the Department of Arts and Entertainment announced its program of action on June 12, 20—. It was no accident that this was the second anniversary not of the murder of Pope (for his elaborately prolonged demise had no precise termination date) but of the discovery of the first "installment" of what later was proved to be his remains. Golden Boy's hand was again evident in this timing. A&E Secretary Apparent Phoenix announced that beginning in the fall, 1200 "units" were to be deleted annually from "all the arts." The number could be adjusted up or down with, and only with, the approval of the secretary or of the vice president, and was subject to annual review. No distinctions were to be made between the arts, which were all to be entered in the same pool, or mix, as it came to be known, and which was to contain: writers (including poets) born *after 1900; artists born after 1875; musicians who recorded after 1950; and all feature films. Television shows, dance, essays and memoirs, and photography were all exempted (some would say excluded) from the pool. When it came to these specifics, members of the Round Table recognized their own work, although of course none of them dared reveal it. Deletions from the mix were adjusted for race and gender, according to a fuzzilogical formula that had been devised by the engine itself. The formula was to be reviewed (but not revised) semiannually by the High Commission, whose own regulations dictated than any review team involving the arts consist of not fewer than three or more than six individuals, with at least two from the "Nations of Color" and no more than one from the US and/or the European Union.*

Chapter 41

It was a gunfight, my first since the raid on the misdemeanor club, and my second altogether. Is it any wonder I was apprehensive going down on the elevator?

"Something smells scary," said Homer, who had opened both big brown eyes, and I had to agree. Still, it seemed more foolish to run from it than to check it out. I had to at least know who was involved and what was at stake.

I could see the flashes as we dropped slowly (but too swiftly!) down. As we got closer to the lobby I could distinguish the *buddha-buddha-buddha* of a Carillon, and the *tak-tak-tak* of a Woodpecker. The Woodpecker made my skin crawl; it was a Woodpecker that had plugged my leg.

"Wait here," I said to Homer as the door clamshelled open. "On second thought, wait upstairs."

I hit twenty-something and stepped out of the elevator. Now I was committed for sure. Just before the door shut, something hit my leg. Too gentle for a bullet. I looked down and saw a single red eye.

The bug. I had forgotten it! How long had it been? I picked it up in tingling fingers, remembering how good it could feel! But I had to concentrate on other things . . .

I jammed it into my pocket and ducked behind a pile of books and tapes. No one had seen me yet, as far as I could tell.

I leaned out to see what was going on.

A wedge of light arced across the floor—so bright it hurt my eyes—*buddha buddha buddha*! There in the open door stood a tiny man with a huge gun, firing out into the parking lot.

It was Lenny.

Buddha buddha buddha!

His father, Panama, stood behind him, firing over his head. *Tak-tak-tak.*

Since no one was shooting at me (or had even noticed me) I straightened up and ran across the floor.

"What's going on?" I asked Panama.

"This is it!" said Panama. "They found us!"

"Who?"

Buddha buddha buddha, answered Lenny's Carillon. It was twice as long as he was, and twice as heavy, but he held it easily, even though the kick sent him skipping backward every time he fired a volley.

Wincing, I peered through the door. The sunlight was blinding. Halfway across the parking lot a body lay in a spreading pool of blood. Behind it I saw black smoke, orange flames. It was the van, burning. As I watched, it exploded in a ball of flames.

"Bob!" I said, reaching out just as Panama shut the door. I jerked my hand back just in time.

"Panama yup Carillon!" said Lenny, resting the weapon on the floor and jamming in a new clip with his knee. "Millennium killer flaps!"

"He's right," said Panama. "It's the Fire Alexandrians. They're here to burn us out."

"How many are there?"

"Hard to tell," he said. "Come on, let's drag this dead one inside where we can question him."

Panama opened the door and Lenny ran out. I followed him. The sunlight was fierce, scorching.

The van had already stopped burning. It was just a smoking heap of twisted metal. It was as if the sun had smothered the fire with its fiercer one.

"Millennium killer flaps!" said Lenny, kneeling over the

body. The dead man looked familiar. But then all dead people look sort of the same.

I went to the van to look for Bob. There was nothing recognizable but the braided wire bones of a steering wheel. The rest was ash and twisted metal too hot to touch. I couldn't get within ten feet.

I turned and saw Lenny dragging the body toward the open door. I followed. Inside, in the dark, I saw why the man had looked familiar. It was Dante. One side of his face had been blown away (the unrifled Carillon fires dum-dum "tumblers") but his unmistakable, unbearable smirk was still there.

I heard a familiar rattling sound. Panama was shaking a sprayette with a hooded monk on it. "What are you doing!?" I asked. "Where did you get that?"

But I knew; Henry kept the LastRites™ in her bra.

"I know this guy," said Panama. "We were partners, friends before the split. Help me out."

It was the last thing I wanted to do, but I did it. I pried Dante's mouth open and held it while Panama sprayed him. Lenny looked on, sitting on the warm Carillon he had been firing only moments before.

"Oh no!" Dante's one remaining eye snapped shut. His hands smacked together and he sat up. "I'm dead, I know it. Don't tell me. I can't stand it."

"You're dead," I said.

"I thought that's what you guys wanted," said Panama.

"Being dead's not the problem," groaned Dante. "It's knowing it."

"You'll burn in Hell," I said.

That seemed to cheer him up. "Hoo fucking ray," he said. "Panama, is that you? Are you ready to burn baby burn?"

"You know it's me, Dante," said Panama. "How did you find us?"

"Ask the pickup artist," said Dante. "Look in his pocket. Next to his dick."

Lenny and Panama were both staring at me. I reached into

my pocket and pulled out the bug. It felt warm and tingly in my fingers.

"You were bugged?" said Panama. He knocked it out of my hand and stepped on it. The tiny *crunch* echoed through the lobby. "You led him here?!"

"This bug was on the van!" I said. I knelt and reached for the pieces, but Panama kicked them away.

I glared up at him. I would have killed him if I could.

"The bug fell in love with him," said Dante. "It was my idea, to crank up the ero-stat. Its learning algorithm unzipped its geo-parameters months ago, and this outlaw bug has been crossing state lines ever since."

"Months?" I stood back up, confused. "I just left New York about a week ago."

"That's what you think," said Dante. "Tell him, Panama."

"I've already told him," said Panama. "In a casino there's no night or day. Vegas time is different."

I looked up at the dark empty space. I could feel the truth of what they were telling me, even though I didn't want to believe them. Had I really missed October rendering? Had all this been for nothing? "How long have I been in here?"

"Eight weeks," said Dante, "and four days. That's when we saw that the bug had stopped traveling and we knew we had the big fish on the line. Now the game is up. Your turn to burn!"

"Are you sure?" asked Panama. "Where are the others?"

"They're right behind me, Panama. Can't have a fire without a library, you know. They're marching with torches. They're singing the Fire Alexandrian song. You'll hear the music any minute now."

"You won't because you'll be dead," I said, as cruelly as I could.

"Hoo fucking ray," he groaned again, his voice a thin whisper. "Do me one favor, Panama, for old time's sake. I have always admired those Vegas crematoriums . . ."

"No favors!" I said.

"It's no big deal," said Panama. "If we leave him outside in the lot the sanibots will pick him up and cremate him. The city pays for it."

"Why do him a favor?" I asked. "He wants to destroy everything you've done. He wants to burn the Millennium down!"

"He's just doing his job," said Panama. "He's an Alexandrian, like me. We used to work together."

"Just like you!" Dante croaked. "Can't have a fire without . . ." Then his one remaining eye popped open and his mouth snapped shut. He fell over on his side, still bent, like a cashew.

Panama reached for the spray. "No, no," I said. I grabbed the sprayette and threw it across the lobby. "That stuff's addictive. Believe me, I know."

Panama closed the dead man's one remaining eye, almost tenderly. He straightened the body; it was already stiffening. Bones and sinews snapped softly. "Dante always had this thing about fire. It's part of being a Fire Alexandrian. Fire and death."

I helped Lenny drag the body back out into the parking lot, for the sanibots. As soon as we got out the door, I saw what they meant about casino time. Even though it had seemed like only minutes had passed, it was dark and the van's ashes were cold. I poked through them and found the urn-mailer. It was undamaged, even to the address bar-code, which I recognized (again, Academy) as somewhere in Wyoming. I filled it with ashes that might have been Bob's, and clicked the little lid shut.

"Millennium box go," said Lenny. He was pointing toward a mailbox at the edge of the parking lot. I dropped the urn-mailer through the slot, which had one wide end.

So long, Bob. Lenny wanted me to pick him up, so I did. He was stronger, and had obviously learned a lot of new words, but he was no bigger than the day he had been born. Up close, I could see that he looked more like his father than his mother. He was bald, and he had a little ponytail. And the tux helped.

"Lennium done," he said. I thought so, too. But we had barely started across the lot toward the door, when we heard a phone ring behind us.

I set Lenny down and he ran (sort of ran) back and got a phone from Dante's pocket. He tried to give it to me, but I shook my head: I didn't want it.

When we got to the door he gave it, still ringing, to Panama.

Panama unfolded the phone and put it to his ear. "It's the old man," he said, handing it to me.

I took it this time. "What old man?" I asked.

Before Panama could answer, a strange, gruff, gravelly voice came on the phone: "Shapiro? The pickup artist?"

"Yes . . ."

"Could I see you upstairs?"

Then a dial tone.

I folded the phone and handed it back to Panama. "What old man? What does he mean, upstairs?"

"I guess you're about to find out."

"Oh man!" said Lenny.

He was pointing across the lobby and up, toward the elevator, which was already heading down to pick me up; empty, except for Homer in her Radio Flyer™.

Chapter 42

*T*he first 1200 units deleted or "pulled" included only fourteen writers who were still read in any numbers; eleven painters whose works appeared in museums and galleries; and twenty-one musicians anyone had heard of at all (though of course, no one remembers them now). The public's fears were put to rest. Everyone (or almost everyone) breathed a sigh of relief: the deletions were going to take from the debris under the orchard of the arts, not from the fruit of the trees. This was of course not true; the branches themselves were to be pruned, but the pruning was to take place over such a long period of time that it was to seem (at least at first) relatively painless. It was never thought that the actual numbers of works deleted would be critical; far more important was the perception that a massive content backlog was being addressed, on a global as well as a local level. This was considered to be enough: the Deletion Option was designed to open the pipeline, freeing the talents and energies of hundreds of thousands of working artists, musicians, poets, and writers. The US government was interested in both the quality and quantity of art produced, which was then the primary component of the gross national product or GNP.

The system was tweaked in the next few years, changed to a hundred deletions a month, listed in an announcement which was itself deleted after one year. There was a contradiction involved in keeping the names of those deleted in a database available to the public, but it was necessary since private copies of books, videos, CDs, etc., were still found in attics and *basements long after the arts themselves had gone digital. Dealing with this fact brought A&E even more public acceptance, with the establishment of the Bureau of Arts and Entertainment, A&E's enforcement and collection arm. Deletion officers (popularly called pickup artists) were needed to retrieve deleted hard copies, so that they wouldn't end up as collector's items in the flee markets which were springing up on state lines around the country to avoid the sales taxes which had been raised to compensate for the abolition of property and income taxes. Hiring more DOs meant that an Academy for recruiting and training had to be established. Enforcement meant more money being pumped into the legal and penal systems. The arts were now a major industry not only in their production, but in their destruction. Cataloging, sales, archiving, and preservation, were now joined (or echoed, some might say) by the parallel activities of uncataloging, unarchiving, and deletion, the last of which alone required armies of personnel for pickup, enforcement, accounting, payment, complaints, and appeals. There were other unintended benefits as well. The applications to A&E's "Art Bank" program, which paid artists a stipend not to produce, were overwhelming, and similar programs were set up in music and literature. The popularity of the Empty Museum in Los Angeles grew exponentially. What was first established as an ironic comment, became a major tourist attraction, as visitors from around the world paid to walk through the empty rooms, looking at the bare walls. In the summer of 20— it outstripped the Getty in the number of visitors. The following year satellite museums were established in Philadelphia and St. Louis, and then Mexico City, Dar es Salaam, and Warsaw. Not the least of the attractions of these museums was the fact that they required no security checks or metal detectors. The deletions also created an underground economy. Since the Deletion Engine was a random device, like those used in state lotteries, it spun off a thriving gambling industry, not only in the market where people bought what*

were (in essence) bootleg futures, but where pools were established on the deletions themselves. Every artist, even those
who were being erased from the canon, found themselves pro-
ducing, if only once, an income stream. Best of all, the admin-
istrative costs of all these programs were paid not by
government but by industry, which was quick to recognize
the enormous financial rewards it gained from periodic
cleansing of the catalog.

The first object of the deletions had been to stimulate the
economy and provide jobs (and secondarily, of course, invig-
orate the arts). The second had been to decrease the violence,
which meant destroy the Alexandrians by making them his-
torically irrelevant. This was even more easily accomplished,
when the government began to do their work for them, and
then to actually pay them for doing the work they had taken
on pro bono as it were. Those copycat or faux Alexandrians
who had been using the movement as a cover for ethnic pride
or ethnic hatred moved on to other projects. The genuine or
original Alexandrians had always been a loose collection,
united only by tactics. Most of them were still unknown,
unidentified even to one another, organized into small cells or
affinity groups or working alone; these were watching and
waiting to see. Others were identified and known—they were
in prison or in jail awaiting trial or sentencing. (And others of
course had been executed.) These were released under a special amnesty (Phoenix Program) and offered jobs in the
Bureau, although this was not made known to the general
public. The unidentified came on board more slowly, but it is
estimated that by 20— over a quarter of the operations and
almost half of the administration of the Bureau was in the
hands of former Fire Alexandrians, "named for the Fire and
not the library." Whether this was Secretary Phoenix's genius
or his folly is still being debated, but the fact is that everyone
was pleased, or at least content, at least for a while. The split
and the new, or Library, Alexandrians came with the debate
around the Immortals.

Chapter 43

*D*ing.
Twenty-five.
The elevator door clamshelled open.

The smell hit me in the face. It was dry and slightly sweet, like the smell of Bob's rug. A death smell. I could hear a faint, distant howling—the pipes of the municipal air conditioning, overworked on this high floor directly assaulted by the merciless Vegas sun.

"Something smells wrong," said Homer.

Pulling the wagon behind me, I stepped out of the elevator and into a dark room, a suite in size, with windows on three sides (drapes all drawn) and the elevator on the fourth.

In the center of the room was a double bed.

In the center of the bed was a man. He lay on his back, looking up at the ceiling.

I took a step closer to the bed.

Ding.

Behind me, the elevator door was closing. Homer and I were alone with the dead man. Because that's what he was, I could see, as soon as I approached the bed. Deader than Bob or Dante had ever been. Dust dead and bone dead.

I walked around him and saw dried leathery skin stretched tight over bones. He wore glasses but he had no nose to perch them on. No eyes. No lips, no ears, and his hair lay in a gray pool like cold gravy around his head on the stained pillow. The smell was faint. I was already used to it. I didn't even have to breathe through my mouth.

Was this the old man who had summoned me? It didn't seem likely, but . . .

"Up here."

It was his voice, but it came from above.

I looked up. That's when I noticed the hole in the ceiling. It was a square, three feet on a side, covered with bars. I hadn't noticed the ladder either. It was in a recess at one side of the elevator.

"There's a key down there," he said in his gravelly voice. "Dresser. Left hand top drawer."

Sure enough, there it was—a big, old-fashioned metal key. I had heard about such keys and even handled one, at Academy.

"And bring the cover."

"The cover?"

"Album cover. The Williams. So we know you are who you say you are."

I hadn't said I was anybody, but I wasn't about to turn back this late in the game. Besides, the album cover part was easy. It was always with me. It rode flat in the Radio Flyer™ underneath Homer. I lifted her just enough to pull it out, surprised and a little alarmed, I think, to see how small and thin her legs and body had become. The album cover was warm, like a living thing.

Which was more than I could say for the old man. And who knew what awaited me up above?

"Wait here," I whispered to Homer. Was it my imagination, or did she nod?

With the album cover under my arm, I climbed halfway up the ladder. I inserted the key into a keyhole at one side of the barred grate that covered the hole.

Nothing happened.

"You have to turn it," said a different voice; a woman's voice.

I turned the key. Nothing happened.

"Now you have to push," she said.

I pushed upward, and sure enough, the grating swung up to one side. I stuck my head up into the room. It wasn't exactly a room; more a garret; or as I was to learn, a cell. It was a four-sided plastic pyramid, about eight feet on a side. The walls arched inward to become the low, pointed roof. A woman in a faded orange jumpsuit lay on her back on a pad on the floor.

"Close the door behind you," she said.

I lowered the steel grate trap back into the floor. It was heavy. Then I straightened up, as best I could, and looked around. I could almost stand in the very middle. The walls were plastic made to look like stone. The narrow cot, the lidless toilet, the tiny sink, all were plastic. The only light came from four long, narrow horizontal slits, each about a meter long, one in each wall.

Finally I forced myself to face her (for it was a woman). She had short gray hair and pale gray skin. Even her eyes were gray. She seemed old but it was hard to tell exactly how old.

I recognized her, of course. "You're Damaris," I said. I had seen her picture at Academy. "I thought you were in prison."

"I am."

"And the man . . . down there?"

"Mr. Bill," she said in the old man's gravely voice. Then she smiled (a cold, thin smile) and switched back to her own. "I'm sure you have heard rumors. I would offer you a seat but as you can see I don't have one. Not even a lid on the toilet."

It was true: I had heard rumors. "That's okay," I said, and squatted down on my heels. Through one of the slits I could see a tiny strip of blue sky, an inch wide and a hundred million light years deep.

"I'm sure you know my history," she said. "Or most of it,

anyway. I know you study it at that Academy."

"We're not allowed to talk about Academy curriculum," I said.

"Don't be ridiculous, Shapiro. You lost your job months ago when you missed Rendering. You have broken every Bureau rule and regulation from the time you pulled the Williams out of your bag. The opening of the bag is a one-way switched plasma membrane with a real-time connection to Enforcement; did you know that?"

"It was a rumor."

"Rumors have a way of being true," she said. "The rumors about the Alexandrians are all true. The rumors about Damaris and Mr. Bill are all true." She had a curious way of talking about herself in the third person at times, and in the plural at others. "We," she would say, or "she." I thought this might be a side effect of the HalfLife™ and of being in solitary confinement for so many years. I think now that it is a more common attribute of celebrity. It's a form of modesty, really; the knowledge that you are even more important to others than you are to yourself, and that your private self casts a shadow across the light from your public self. I sat back on my heels in one corner of Damaris's cell while she told me her story, which was the story of the Alexandrians, which was also the story of the man below us.

I gradually got used to her voice. It was like a recording that had been slowed down. Which in a way it was. The HalfLife™ slowed her down and, as I was beginning (slowly!) to understand, the casino slowed the rest of us. It was almost a match; it made her seem almost, if not quite, normal. She told me that Mr. Bill had hired her . . .

"Hired you?!"

"Don't interrupt."

. . . before he had actually met her. He knew her of course from her films, but he was not a fan, much less a lover. That came later. This was strictly business. He needed a star, any star, and when he learned of her suicide attempt . . .

"Suicide?!"

"Terminex™ and Absolut™ vodka. I was almost sixty years old and I hadn't had been offered a part or been in a magazine for twelve years. Now please don't interrupt."

. . . he guessed correctly at the source of her despair, and dispatched his attorneys in their fleet of dark cars, and offered her a starring role, her last, that would assure her place in legend and history. It was an offer she could, but didn't, refuse. A major part, her final role.

In playing an Alexandrian Damaris would be playing a role Mr. Bill himself had helped to write. For as he revealed to her later, he had financed the first efforts of the Alexandrians in the U.S. Mr. Bill had become rich by digitizing books and film, then moving into music and art. He was among the first to see how the ever-growing past must dilute the value of the future. The trend was, had to be, downward. The only surprising thing to him was that no one else had noticed it. When the "Eliminateurs" made their first attacks in France he was thrilled, even though they clearly had their own agenda. He liked the fact that their attacks were on art, for only in art does the original have an intrinsic value. Destroying the unreproducible excited Mr. Bill, even though for him the ultimate target was film, music, books. His bread and butter.

And he liked their secrecy. Not only did it have a natural appeal for a man whose private awkwardness was legendary: the anarchic and shadowy Alexandrian underground was an arena in which he, or indeed anyone with imagination or money, or both, could move. Mr. Bill funded a number of small groups in the U.S., never of course actually taking part himself.

"No one could tie Mr. Bill to the Getty explosion," Damaris said. "But from the first arrests he saw the opportunity to begin the process of turning private protest into public policy." She was easily added to the Getty list through a private Papal connection. The police wanted arrests, not certainty. "I wanted two things," she said, "death and immortality, and I was offered both. Is it any wonder that I strove to make my last role my greatest?"

"And did you actually believe any of it?"

"Of course. Though I'm a Californian, I studied in Hell's Kitchen. An actor trained in the Method grows into a role. I grew to believe. I grew to love my codefendants. I was sincerely trying to save their lives, and ended up saving only my own. I persuaded Mr. Bill to finance my appeals, not only because I was horrified by my sentence—I had sought death, not HalfLife™!—but because I wanted to do what I could to make sure the Alexandrian vision lived on after I was gone."

Her voice grew thoughtful. "Or perhaps it's the same thing. It was my greatest role and I wasn't ready to give it up."

The approach prison in which Damaris was held during appeals was a private institution easily acquired by one of Mr. Bill's companies (the first of many such acquisitions) thus allowing him to wire her into the Round Table without directly breaking penal codes. This was important to her. Like most Hollywood stars who believe their celebrity is deserved, she was adamantly opposed to cheating.

"The Round Table," said Damaris, "was my curtain call. A final appearance as the icon of deletion, the minus angel, the null queen. The problem was, as we began to develop the deletion protocols that later were enshrined in your own Bureau, I, who still yearned for death, began to see and understand the horror of it."

"The horror?"

"The horror. I could accept the death of the individual but not of the work of art."

While she talked, always in her own whispery voice, I looked around the tiny cell. One of the slots was turning red. She didn't seem to mind, or even notice, when I got up. Through the slot I saw for the first time all (or a quarter, or almost a third) of Vegas, the towers just being lit like candles, the endless stream of circling lectros. No people, not as part of the visible world, anyway. They were inside the casinos and attractions, or inside the cars and lectros streaming to and from the casinos and attractions. It was almost dark. It was the universe as I had always imagined it, too grand for humans to behold except at night, and then only in silence. I wondered if Damaris had ever looked out these slits. They were the only windows in the casino. Through them to the west was a wall of mountains, with snow that moved up and down as swiftly (it seemed) as cloud shadows. To the east, north, and south I saw only desert with dry mountains in scattered piles, like old droppings.

He dimmed me out. He betrayed me. He falsified my last statement and dimmed me out. I was no longer his ally, but I was still his prisoner."

Literally. Mr. Bill owned the entire prison system, which had been privatized piece by piece, by the time Damaris's appeals were exhausted and she was sealed into her cell by The Loved Ones, Inc. Her sentence was reconfirmed: nineteen consecutive life terms, plus a fifty-year appeal penalty, without, by special legislation, the *possibility* of the possibility of parole. It was the harshest sentence ever imposed on a Celebrity in the continental U.S. "And the funny thing was, by the time it happened, I was glad. HalfLife™ is not death but it's close; it removes you from the world. Though not, as it turned out, from Mr. Bill."

Chapter 44

*I*t is remarkable, indeed amazing, how many working artists, writers, poets, musicians, etc., can be deleted before a name comes up that is known to the public at large. On August 11, 20— John Steinbeck was pulled, as one of the hundred for that week. Here for the first time was a Nobel Prize winner. The mutterings in the Bureau, and above, in the faux-walnut-paneled halls of A&E, were soon picked up by the "press," and not long afterward by the letters columns and the talk shows. It was not about Steinbeck, who was no more widely read in 20— than when he had died. But a name that everyone knew reminded everyone that there were names that everyone cared about. What if it were Frank Sinatra? Or Toni Morrison? Or Pope himself, whose thousand "page" novels were more popular now than ever, in spite of (or perhaps because of) his protracted and ghastly demise. Should not certain Immortals be secured in the canon, not subject to deletion?

Thus the question that had first split the Round Table found its way inexorably into the bureaucracy, and ultimately into the public discourse, such as it was. Random deletion was too extreme, it was said, too harsh; there needed to be a few Immortals to temper its effects and give continuity to humanity, or at least humanity's dreams. There were already Immortals, was the reply: Mozart, Shakespeare, even Hemingway (who was born in 1899). Every generation needed its own Immortals, said one voice. Every generation needed its own space, replied another. Besides, who would choose the Immortals? And who would *choose the choosers? To bypass or overrule random selection even in a few instances would open a Pandora's box of political agendas, both acknowledged and hidden, dictated by class, race, gender. So the debate raged—a little among the public, which was only peripherally concerned; more among the academics and the "press," both of which were always looking for material; and most of all among the Alexandrians hidden (in plain view) in the Bureau and the Department.*

Trade was the determinant. While Elvis and Morrison might seem universal to the American point of view, they were far less important in the world context; and it was the WTO that had ultimate authority over the Department, the Bureau, and its progams. The concept of Immortals was rejected and declared illegal; no one wanted to decide who would decide. The debate was ended; the talk died down. Or so it seemed. But a more heated if hidden discussion was going on underground, like a smoldering fire in the forest that flames up when there's no one around. Questions were asked; new contacts were made; old ones renewed. Quietly, people came together, calling themselves Library Alexandrians ("named after the library and not the fire"). Unable to agree on which Immortals to save, they decided to save them all, forming a negative canon consisting of everything that the Bureau deleted. Their first efforts were electronic, but since these are easily detected and erased, they moved into the hard copy realm, which required alliances with various aspects of the underworld that had become the bootleggers. This required money, which brought an unexpected ally into the mix.

"Mr. Bill," I said.

"I had won him over at last," said Damaris. "He fell in love."

Chapter 45

Love takes many forms," said Damaris. "Mr. Bill told me later that he spent hours, then days, then weeks at a time watching me as I lay like Sleeping Beauty in my narrow cell. Wishing he could bring me back to life. Wishing he could apologize, and wishing is a kind of love. So is worship. Movie Stars (and I was still a Movie Star) can sense such things, even through the slow haze of HalfLife™, in which a year seems but a minute, and a minute a year.

"The horror I had felt at the Round Table hit him gradually as my films were deleted, one by one. I was disappearing. Once they were gone I would be only a convict, less than a woman, really. No longer a Movie Star. Meanwhile the Alexandrians were reforming, dedicated to preserving rather than destroying art. Still illegal, still clandestine, still secret. Mr. Bill began working behind the scenes, financing them and pulling them together, until a parallel shadow organization had been built—the Library Alexandrians, named for the library, not the fire."

"So he financed them both."

"One to please himself and one to please me," she said. "Or so he thought. With the HalfLife™ I had long since ceased to care. Though I never told him that. By then he had acquired the casino and gaming industries, and with it the technology that allowed us to communicate, even talk, even (and this was strange but wonderful) touch. He moved here, then moved me here. We were on casino time, as indeed lovers often are. Was it years we had together . . . or was it only days?"

The question was not directed at me. I waited long minutes—or was it hours?—in silence, until she spoke again.

"Since he died, I have been running things. Mostly the casinos, plus a mine or two, a car rental company—Thrifty, I think. And of course, Corrections." She opened one hand to show me the cell phone clutched against her still-generous breast.

"His voice," I said.

"I'm an actor. He's an eccentric, a recluse. Piece of cake."

"That makes you your own warden," I said. "Why don't you let yourself go?" I held out the key (even though the grate through which I had ascended was still unlocked).

She shrank back as if from a flame. "The world holds only horror for me. It is all excess. I want only to get farther from it, not closer. Especially now that Mr. Bill is gone."

"Then why don't you take yourself off the HalfLife™?"

"I did, long ago," she said. "Right after he died. I was jealous; I wanted to follow him. Unfortunately, HalfLife™ lodges in the tissues."

"Like dioxin."

"How did you know? But all that is unimportant. What we built is what will free me. What will free me is love."

"Love?"

"The bug. Surely you remember the little lovesick bug."

I told her what had happened. My eyes suddenly brimmed with what might have been tears, but they were gone before I could be sure.

"It's okay," she said. "Its death confirmed its life. The important thing is, the Bureau bugged you, knowing you had taken the Williams out of the bag, not knowing that the Fire Alexandrians had bugged the Bureau."

"And you let them?" I was shocked. "Even though you know they intend to destroy everything the Library Alexandrians have saved?"

"You can't have a fire without a library," she said. "Life without death, freedom without prison, beginnings without ends. Once I heard they were on their way, I knew the circle was about to close."

And suddenly I understood. This was her escape. The Fire Alexandrians were coming to set her free. The red through the slit, like a bar of fire, seemed to confirm it. The sunset slit.

"They are coming to burn the place down," I said again. "They will destroy it all."

"Not necessarily. Not all." She smiled. "You are a pickup artist, are you not? Then get to work. You have a day, a week, maybe even a month. Choose your Immortals, get them to the dock. The Bobs will take them out."

"Where?"

"Is that your concern? Has that ever been your concern? The Bobs have agreed to put them back into the mix, where they will have to take their chances with everything else. The flee markets. The bootleggers. Who knows."

I saw my chance. "I would have to start with the Williams."

"I anticipated that," she said. "I had Lenny watch for it. And guess what?"

She held out her empty hand, and I thought I was being taunted. Then I realized what she wanted, and handed her the album cover.

She reached under her mattress and pulled out a record, still in its little paper sleeve, and slipped it into the album cover, a sleeve within a sleeve.

"There." She handed it back to me, then spoke in the old man's gravelly voice:

"Now. Go, and do what you were trained to do. Do what you came here to do. There will be Immortals. How many and who they are depends on how much you get done before the Fire Alexandrians get here."

"What makes them Immortal then?"

"Immortal just means they get a second chance."

I was doubtful. But I had always had my doubts, and had never let them interfere with my job.

I reached out to shake her hand but she had already turned away on her bed. I got up to go. I raised the grate, then stopped and looked back at Damaris, the legendary Movie Star, the icon of the Alexandrians, Library and Fire, for what turned out to be the last time. All I saw was her back.

"One other thing I need," I said. "A record-player."

"What the hell," she asked, in Mr. Bill's voice, without turning over, "is a record-player?"

Chapter 46

W hat the hell's a record-player?" asked Panama.

I started to describe it. Then I saw by his narrow eyes that he was kidding; it was his idea of a joke. He took me to a room off the loading dock where items left in the upper rooms had been stored. The record-player was exactly like the one I had seen at Charlie Rose High in Brooklyn; exactly like the one I had gone to the misdemeanor club to buy. All that seemed so long ago. It was magenta and gray, gray that reminded me of ashes, ashes that reminded me of Bob, Bob whom I dropped in the mail—how long ago?

It fit into the Radio Flyer™ just right, turned up on its side. I didn't even have to take Homer out. Her hindquarters, and indeed her entire body had shrunk almost to nothing, as her head had gotten larger. It was like a squirrel's body attached to the head of a horse. It didn't bother me, though. She was still with me: that was the important thing.

The album (no longer just the album cover) fit in the wagon, too. So did Lenny, always looking for a ride.

It was day outside, according to the bar of light under the door. The loading dock was the only place in the Millennium where it was possible to tell day from night.

I went out to the lobby and pressed the button for the elevator, then pressed 19. It seemed appropriate that Henry should hear the record, too. I sat on the bed beside Henry and closed my eyes when the music started, and sure enough, I could see my father standing in the doorway in his cowboy hat. I could smell his cigarette, and the gas-o-line (I knew, now, that was what it was) on his hands. I knew at last what he had been about to say, for he said it now, in a voice that sounded a lot like Homer's: "You take care of the dog, son, it's time for me to hit the road."

The record went *tik-tik-tik* when it was over. When I opened my eyes Henry was still asleep but Panama was standing in the hard world doorway, listening, too.

"Find what you were looking for?"

"None of your business," I said. But I had.

That was the last I saw of Panama, which was fine with me. I saw a lot more of Lenny. He liked to ride the elevators; he liked to ride in the Radio Flyer™ as well. He could no longer ride on Homer's back, like a cowboy, so he rode on the wagon rim, crossing his legs. It made him look sophisticated, like a Fred Astaire doll.

Fred Astaire is one of the Immortals, whatever that means. I guess it just means he gets another chance. Lenny picked him out. So is Hank Williams, of course. I listened to the record once more, then put it on the dock. The next morning (whatever that means) he was gone.

So I was a pickup artist again. It felt good. With Lenny's help, and Homer in tow, I scoured the hotel for "Immortals," choosing one I knew and one I didn't from each room, in an effort to be fair.

Sometimes when I put my hand in my pocket I missed the bug. But only a little.

It was Lenny who found the second Williams. We had covered every room in the Millennium and we were starting over, and I was surprised I hadn't seen it before. But it was Hank Williams all right, the same songs in a slightly different order. Instead of taking it to the dock we left it by Henry's bed, so that we could stop by from time to time and listen. We stopped by from time to time and every time it was the same: Henry asleep, her arms outside the sheets, her bluebird sweater folded on the pillow beside her.

Every time it was the same for me, too: I turn to the door (with my eyes closed) and there, not in real life, but in my imagination, is the old man himself, but young—not as old as I am now (how old am I now?) but young, in the way that those who died young long ago are forever young. An Immortal in his own mysterious way.

I was afraid of running into Panama, at first, but Henry was always by herself, like a sleeping beauty in her bluebird bra.

Fortunately, or unfortunately, as the case may be, there's a last time for everything. Lenny and I had just dropped a load at the dock, when he pulled at my sleeve, and said "Hank up," and I heard it, too.

The record was playing far above, on nineteen. But it didn't sound quite right. We took the elevator up. Someone (Panama? Henry?) had started the record-player but the "needle" had picked up a ball of dust that was causing it to jump back and repeat the same groove over over and over.

"So lonesome I . . .

"So lonesome I . . .

"So lonesome I . . ."

I fixed it (by blowing on it) and started the record at the beginning. They play from the outside in. Lenny sat on his mother's bed, legs crossed, Fred Astaire style. Homer's big brown eyes were closed; they had been closed for "days." I closed mine as soon as the scratchy voice started to sing, and there he was in the doorway again, hat on, just like Hank.

Then I heard a shout, and I opened my eyes, and he was gone. Lenny was standing up, pulling at Henry's hair and bra strap. I could hear shouts from far below, whoops and hollers.

Henry was awake at last. She sat up, eyes wide, knocking

Lenny away and clutching the coverlet to her breast. The needle was *click-click-click*ing in its groove, stuck again:

"So lonesome I . . .

"So lonesome I . . ."

I could hear laughter from far below, and what might have been singing. Footsteps, running. Breaking glass.

"Something smells wonderful," said Homer. "Time to hit the road."

I could smell it, too. That capacious, elegant, ballroom gas-o-line smell like doors opening in the mind. And underneath it, something else.

Smoke.

Chapter 47

Everybody has one thing they keep, one thing that matters to them more than anything else. Life is just a process of elimination, figuring out what that one thing is. You figure it out at the end, just as you're losing it—

If you're lucky (and I've always been lucky).

I knew from Academy drills not to take the elevator. The smoke was already filling the great central shaft of the Millennium. I was halfway down the stairs with Homer in my arms before I realized I had left the album and the record-player and the Radio Flyer™ behind, not to mention Henry and Lenny. But I needn't have worried. They were waiting for me at the door. They had taken the elevator.

"That dog's dead," said Henry as we followed Lenny out the door, into the staggering sunlight. Lenny was pulling the wagon. Henry was carrying her sweater in one hand and the album in the other. I thought she had rescued it but then I saw it was only the cover.

"Just barely," I said, as I put Homer into the wagon. Her body was as small and limp as a sock. "She saved our lives."

"Yours, maybe," said Henry. "I saved mine."

Homer was gone. Her eyes were wide open. I closed them with my fingertips, then checked my own. Those were definitely tears. I blinked and looked off at the horizon, the way they do in the movies. I would have, should have, marked the date but there was no way, in Vegas, to tell. The snow on the mountains could mean either spring or summer; the seasons here were not like the seasons on Staten Island, measured by living things. Here there were only elements: rock, snow, sand, glass, and pavement.

Lenny pulled Homer inside and put the wagon on the elevator and sent her up. A regular Viking funeral. I was still crying when he returned, but only a little. I felt somehow free. It was an alarming feeling.

Henry still hadn't put on her sweater. Maybe it was the heat. "Where's Panama?" I asked, more to be polite than anything; so it wouldn't seem I was staring.

She shrugged. The bluebirds all shrugged, too.

"Panama Millennium yup!" said Lenny, pointing up toward the top of the building, which was glowing either with sun or a nearer, hotter fire, it was hard to tell.

"Time to hit the road," said Henry, throwing her sweater over one shoulder like a tramp. Windows were popping from the heat, cascading down into the parking lot. We were backing away, into the street, when a truck pulled up, a sleek new Nabisco. A familiar face peered out.

"Aren't you the pickup artist?" Indian Bob asked, eyeing my sky blue, one-stripe pants. "Which way you going?"

"West," said Henry.

"Yup!" said Lenny.

Who was I to disagree?